Born in the Royal Military Hospital in Portsmouth, England, in 1938, he attended Titchfield Primary School (Hampshire, UK) and Fareham Secondary Modern Boys School (Hampshire, UK) until 1953.

Joining the Royal Air Force as an apprentice in 1955, he served 14 years and was discharged in 1968. During that period, he met and married Kim in 1962, and they are still together 58 years later. After a short period as a prison officer, he entered the computer industry with Golden Wonder Ltd. and stayed in that profession with various companies until 1991. He then joined an inner-city medical practice in Leicester (Leicestershire, UK) as fundholding manager and practice manager until his retirement in 2003. After spending thirteen years dividing his time between his home in Leicester and Sax, a small town near Alicante in Spain, he has now moved permanently back to the UK and lives in Oadby, Leicestershire.

I dedicate this book to Bethany. She was a ten-year-old young lady at the time of the first publication (2011), who read the book and picked up spelling and grammatical errors that I missed (despite me having re-read it numerous times). She also did me the honour of commenting on various sections in a most favourable and constructive way, with some of her comments resulting in small parts being rewritten.

Robert A.V. Jacobs

DAISY WEAL

AUSTIN MACAULEY PUBLISHERS™
LONDON • CAMBRIDGE • NEW YORK • SHARJAH

Copyright © Robert A.V. Jacobs (2021)

The right of Robert A.V. Jacobs to be identified as author of this work has been asserted by the author in accordance with section 77 and 78 of the Copyright, Designs and Patents Act 1988.

All rights reserved. No part of this publication may be reproduced, stored in a retrieval system, or transmitted in any form or by any means, electronic, mechanical, photocopying, recording, or otherwise, without the prior permission of the publishers.

Any person who commits any unauthorised act in relation to this publication may be liable to criminal prosecution and civil claims for damages.

This is a work of fiction. Names, characters, businesses, places, events, locales, and incidents are either the products of the author's imagination or used in a fictitious manner. Any resemblance to actual persons, living or dead, or actual events is purely coincidental.

A CIP catalogue record for this title is available from the British Library.

ISBN 9781398407763 (Paperback)
ISBN 9781398415027 (Hardback)
ISBN 9781398407794 (ePub e-book)
ISBN 9781398407787 (Audiobook)

www.austinmacauley.com

First Published (2021)
Austin Macauley Publishers Ltd
25 Canada Square
Canary Wharf
London
E14 5LQ

I would like to thank my wife, Kim, for her considerable support, encouragement and tendency to refer to Daisy as someone 'real'. Without her, the book would probably never have been written, and whether or not that would have been a good thing, only history will tell. Special thanks go to my sister for introducing the unpublished manuscript to a young man by the name of Ethan Crowson, aged eleven, who took the time to read it and more importantly liked it. Thank you also to my daughter-in-law, Arla, from Finland for reading each chapter emailed to her, impatiently demanding the next and insisting that I include Finland somewhere in the story.

Other Works by the Author

Children's fiction, ten years upwards

Daisy Weal and the Monster
Daisy Weal and Sir Charles
Daisy Weal and the Last Crenian
Dauntless
The Lost Starship
The Star Queen
The Adventures of Daisy Weal (Omnibus edition, containing four of the books in the series)
Grandpa's Shed
Cindy Lost and the Black Witch

Short stories in the Daisy Weal series (Available as e-books):

Daisy Weal and the Grelflin
Daisy Weal and the Weenies
Daisy Weal and the Millions
Daisy Weal and the Face
Daisy Weal and the Secret
Daisy Weal and the Disaster
Daisy Weal and the Ghost

Daisy Weal and the Figment

Young adult and adult fiction:

Speaker (A collection of 29 short stories)
The Yellow Dragon
The Diamond Sword of Tor
Cardoney (Omnibus edition containing both The Yellow Dragon and The Diamond Sword of Tor)

Adult science fiction:

As a Consequence
Taldi'na
With No Warning

Adult detective/murder mysteries:

Dexxman
The Disappearance of Natalie Firth
Time to Die
A Promise to Doreen
Almost Enough
The Eighteenth Panda
The Seventh Tower
The Ordeal

Non-fiction:

Sudoku, Food for the Mind

Author's Note

Some years ago, I wrote part of the first chapter of this book, and the last chapter. My only problem became what to put in between. The embryo masterpiece languished as a tiny Word document, lost amongst many other files, and passing from Computer to Computer as I upgraded over the years.

There came a time, however, when the trip of a lifetime was planned, a journey around the world visiting New York, Los Angeles, Hawaii, Fiji, New Zealand, Australia and Singapore.

I loaded everything I thought I would need onto my laptop and together with my wife, Kim, embarked on the first stage of our trip from Heathrow to New York. It was during that flight that I discovered a small file on my laptop and was once again reunited with Daisy Weal, and the rest of her story began to form.

I sent an email to J.K. Rowling's agent, Christopher Little, saying that I intended to make a reference to Hogwarts and that if they objected, to please email me. I received no reply. So for the implied agreement in their silence, I say thank you.

There are a number of apologies that I should make to ensure that the record is as straight as it possibly could be, with the first going to Brighton. I apologise profusely to

Brighton for intimating that no one would want to go there. I could have used any coastal town, but unfortunately, none of them have a Brighton Pavilion. I apologise to the legal systems of Spain, Ireland, Canada and the United Kingdom, for the simple reason that I may want to visit them one day. No offence was intended. Finally, I apologise to NASA for making fun of their Mission Control in such a brief way; I should have spent more time on it.

I don't apologise for using New York as it really is the biggest city in the world that you can't get lost in. My only wish is that the authorities in that great city would humour me and install a brand-new rubbish bin on the corner of Sixth Avenue and Fifty-Sixth Street and paint a screaming face on it.

Character List

Though not all of these characters appear in this book, they are those that run through Daisy's life.

Alfie: Daisy's friend, lives in Oak Place.

Candy-Anne: Daisy's friend, lives in Hawaii.

Carson, Harriet Annabelle: Marjorie's sister, married to Robert Carson. Lives in Canada.

Carson, Robert: English structural engineer, based in Canada and married to Harriet.

Chase, Brett: Astronaut, the third member of the Luna mission, also lives remotely…not far from Chuck Landers.

Connors, Nate: Astronaut and second in command of the Luna mission, now lives not far from Chuck Landers.

Correo, Alfred: Local postman, briefly the most wanted man in three countries.

D'Arco, Jimmie: Daisy and Alfie's friend and environmental assassin, lives at sixteen Cross Street.

Drake, Joe: The milkman, the only human thus far, other than Daisy, to have visited an 'in-between' place.

Franks, Cedric: Last man in the world to have long yellow ears.

Flaunt, Suzy: Plumber's girlfriend, but briefly suspected of running away with the milkman. Lives in Povey Street.

Foster, Cyril: Scruffy, tall and lanky, a senior manager at George's place of work.

Frogget, Angela: Wannabe witch, married to Mark.

Frogget, Mark: Wannabe witch, married to Angela, both live at thirty-two Trendal Place.

Frogget, Michael: Only child of Mark and Angela.

Kilpatrick, Colin: An Irishman, manager of the local supermarket and Daisy's next-door neighbour at number ten.

Landers, Chuck: Astronaut and commander of the Luna mission. Lives on a remote farm in America and believes Daisy to be a figment of his imagination.

Landers, Mavis: Chuck Landers' wife.

Madsen, Mike: Corner shop owner, local interrogator. His shop is on the corner of Trendal Place.

Martin, Andrew: Arch villain and dog hater, ex-owner of Bruce and lives at twenty-five Trendal Place.

Old, Gary: Owner of an antique shop called 'Old Antiques' in Bishop's Ashton.

Old John: Local drunk.

Prentice, Arthur: An accountant and Daisy's next-door neighbour at number fourteen.
Reynolds, Jasper: A farmer who thinks poltergeists plough his fields, but keeps it quiet in case they stop.

Somethings: A composite being, supposedly created as a control on the Vana, capable of influencing very small things, can be very irritating.

Swain, Jack: Unpleasant child, who is reformed by Daisy. Lives at twenty-two Ingle Road.

Swain, James: Bother of Jack, also unpleasant and also reformed by Daisy, and also lives at twenty-two Ingle Road.

Trent, Gladys, Mrs (Mrs Trentovovich): Russian spy living at number 16 Trendal Place, who apparently entered the European Union through Finland.

Vanaelcrocedus (Vana): A composite being from the dawn of time, of immense power.

Weal, Daisy: The heroine of our story. A young lady, gifted with extraordinary powers, who lives at twelve Trendal Place.

Weal, George: Father to Daisy, husband to Marjorie.

Weal, Marjorie: Mother to Daisy, wife to George.

Weal, Millicent Daisy: Daisy's grandmother and George's mother, lived just outside Waikiki in Hawaii before moving to twelve Trendal Place.

Table of Contents

Foreword	1
Chapter One: Definitely the Oddest of Places	2
Chapter Two: Does Liquorice Grow on Trees?	10
Chapter Three: Where Art Thou Milkman?	16
Chapter Four: The Hole That Jack Built	23
Chapter Five: Does Being Green Help the Environment?	29
Chapter Six: Daisy and Her Namesake	34
Chapter Seven: A Postman's Holiday	40
Chapter Eight: Odd Things Happen in Brighton	46
Chapter Nine: Is the Moon a Nice Place to Live?	53
Chapter Ten: Some Things Are Best Forgotten	58
Chapter Eleven: Aunt Harriet	64
Chapter Twelve: Burglars and Trendal Place	70
Chapter Thirteen: Once Bitten	76
Chapter Fourteen: Of Witches and Warlocks	84

Chapter Fifteen: A Record for George	91
Chapter Sixteen: Revelation	98
Chapter Seventeen: 'Bin' to New York	107
Chapter Eighteen: Where Is Coventry?	116
Chapter Nineteen: Grandma's Broke	122
Chapter Twenty: Making Things Right (1)	132
Chapter Twenty-One: Making Things Right (2)	139
Chapter Twenty-Two: Loose Ends	146
Chapter Twenty-Three: Home	151
Excerpt from Book 2: *Daisy Weal and the Monster*	156
Chapter One: The Invasion	

Foreword

Daisy Weal lived a normal life, right up until the moment she was born. Then things went downhill…

Now one little girl must face the reality that she could do things that others couldn't and discover how dangerous it could be if they found out. So her early years were spent learning to control her gifts, trying to fit in, to be human. It wasn't easy. There were mistakes…big mistakes, some of which couldn't be made right.

But she isn't as alone as she thinks. She forms an inseparable bond with a very large dog named Bruce. Together, they will face the world and discover that as much as Daisy has tried to fit in, it might ultimately be impossible.

Should she accept that she is not completely human or fully embrace the part of her that is?

Chapter One
Definitely the Oddest of Places

It started as a fairly unassuming day at 12 Trendal Place, Bishop's Ashton. The sun was trying hard to break through a grey misty sky, with limited success. It had been raining on and off for a number of days and everything was damp and glistening in the hazy sunshine. A slight breeze ruffled the still wet, lush green lawns, which had grown at least six inches since they had last received attention. Everything had taken on a dark and leaden feeling, and the silence hung hard in the street and surrounding areas, waiting with bated breath it seemed, for the inevitable sounds of lawn mowers and strimmers to intrude into this all too brief period of tranquillity.

In the distance towards the town centre, the sounds of life were more normal, with the noise of traffic and the occasional horn's 'beep' from an impatient motorist, wafting in on the slight movement of air. A large aircraft passed overhead, out of sight in the sky, its engines in full voice as it gained height from the nearby international airport. *Probably off to some exotic place*, thought Marjorie Weal as she stood in her doorway to take a deep breath of the cool and damp morning air. Against the cold, she had pulled on a coat over her nightdress, but had kept on her slippers, rightly considering that being large, fluffy and pink, they would be warmer than shoes. She leaned against the doorframe, waiting for the milkman and wishing that her pregnancy was over. *Nine months is too long*, she thought and then giggled to herself, *Women should have been designed with three months in mind.*

A milk float whined to a stop at the head of the street and the clink of bottles broke the silence as the milkman began his deliveries. He muttered, "Pig of a mornin', innit," as he stood aside at the gate of number ten to let the postman pass and then followed him up the path to the front door.

"Yeh, but the sun keeps trying," was returned.

Marjorie walked slowly down the few metres to her front gate to wait for the postman as he came out of next door and was greeted with:

"Mornin', Ms Weal, nothing today, I'm afraid; would only have been bills anyway. Baby due soon? Have you thought of a name yet?"

"Very soon, thank you, but not today, I hope," observed Marjorie. "Well, if it's a girl, we're calling her Daisy; haven't made up our mind if it's a boy."

"Well, you take yourself inside. It's no day for you to be out and about in your condition. Don't you agree, Joe?" The postman nodded to the Milkman as he approached.

Joe handed two bottles of half-fat pasteurised milk to Marjorie and said, "You do as the man says, Ms Weal. He should know; he's got six kids."

Marjorie nodded and then turned and walked towards her front door. She had only walked a couple of paces when the first contraction hit. "Oh, George," she gasped as she doubled over. The pains became intense and rapid and she dropped to her knees; the two bottles of milk fell from her hands and rolled down the path as she grabbed her stomach.

"You see to her, I'll get Mr Weal," said Joe, ignoring the rolling bottles as he vaulted over Marjorie and rushed to the front door.

"Mr Weal, Mr Weal," he shouted through the open door.

It all became a blur for Marjorie after that. All she knew was that the pains were too close. There had been no build up and it was all too sudden. Then George was kneeling beside her and taking her hand.

"Hang on, the ambulance is on its way; you'll be OK," and then, "I hope!" she heard him mutter under his breath.

Then the ambulance arrived and it seemed that they were at the hospital almost instantly. Before she knew it, she was being manhandled onto a stretcher, lights were rushing past, a nurse appeared and the pain stopped.

Through bleary eyes, she saw the doctor approaching with a bundle in his hands.

"It's a girl," he grinned and turned the bundle to face Marjorie. All she could see was an enormous set of green eyes looking at her from this wonderful little face. The eyes turned and looked straight at her.

"Well, I'm glad that's over," said Daisy.

The nurse folded in on herself and crumpled to the ground. The doctor threw Daisy straight up into the air as he fainted and fell over backwards, knocking trolleys and instruments in all directions. Marjorie, being made of sterner stuff, just went to sleep again. Somehow, Daisy had landed in the crib the right way round and perfectly centred. She gurgled happily to herself because, after all, she was a baby.

This is definitely the oddest of places, she thought. Then the door flew open and more people rushed in.

"What has happened here?" demanded a very stern-looking nurse.

"Oh, they all fainted," said Daisy.

Three more people joined the heap on the floor. But the stern-looking nurse, who had not been looking at Daisy, swivelled around with eyes that were deep, dark and accusing. That gaze was obviously designed to reduce lesser nurses to jelly, and from the fear on the faces of the others, it was very effective indeed.

"Who said that?" she bellowed.

"Now, now," muttered Marjorie, who had still not quite woken up but had been disturbed by the racket, "not so much noise, you'll frighten the baby. I suggest that you get some help to remove all these fainted bodies. I do declare that people will fall over at the drop of a hat these days."

The nurse took one more look around, swivelled about and swept from the room.

"Hello Mum," said Daisy.

Marjorie, being full of gas and air, which apparently is given to aid difficult births, was so convinced that she was hallucinating that she thought she would play along with her imagination for a little while, or at least until the effects wore off. So, dreamily, she said, "This really is something that I have to get my head around but, in the meantime, dear, please remember that you are a baby, and until we are alone, you only know how to gurgle. Babies don't speak for at least a couple of years."

"How odd," said Daisy, "can I talk to Dad?"

"Not a good idea. Having a baby is hard enough on the poor dear, but one that talks might be too much. I think it would be better if we kept this as our little secret for the time being. Now shush, someone is coming," replied Marjorie, realising at last that this was indeed real, and that she was neither hallucinating nor dreaming.

The bodies were removed, revived and sent somewhere to 'rest until they were feeling better'. A pair of security guards walked up and stationed themselves at her door and then people in suits started to appear. They were milling around, talking heatedly and pausing periodically to look towards Marjorie. Then, one important-looking man removed himself from the mêlée and strode purposefully towards her door.

"I understand that your baby spoke—" he started to say.

"Do you?" interrupted Marjorie, who by now had virtually recovered from her medications. She knew that to prevent unwanted intrusion into her life and that of her new baby, she would have to quickly take control of the situation.

"Then you are a bigger fool than you look. Here she is, no more than an hour old," she continued, trying desperately not to laugh and, at the same time, sound sarcastic,

"Go on, look; she won't bite. Does she look as if she can speak? Or is the word of a group of people, who have trouble remaining conscious, of paramount importance here?"

"I have—" he tried again.

"No, you don't," said Marjorie, interrupting him again. "What you have to do is look at my baby, then remove yourself and the guards and let us get some rest. Oh, and find my husband, he must be worried sick."

The man looked confused and about to say something else, but instead, he bent over the crib and said, "Hello," to Daisy.

Daisy stared up at him, smiled happily, dribbled a little and said, "Goo."

The rest of the stay in the hospital was fairly uneventful, with the normal comings and goings of a busy maternity unit. The members of staff who had attended her in the beginning and then had been carried out didn't appear in the department again. So, for a little while, no one had time for any pleasantries until replacements were found. There were still whispers and quick glances towards her, but no one bothered her.

George came in as often as his work would allow and then sat holding Marjorie's hand, staring at the baby for hours on end. Sometimes, he arrived so tired that he fell asleep with his head cradled in Marjorie's arms.

"He is so tired," whispered Daisy.

"He's a good man, Daisy," said Marjorie, "who wants to make a good life for us. He works too hard, so I think we can let him sleep for a while."

Those enormous green eyes stared silently at Marjorie for a few seconds.

"You were expecting me before you married him, weren't you?" asked Daisy.

There was no accusation in the voice or in the eyes. It was just a question that Marjorie wished hadn't been asked, but now that it had, it could not be avoided.

"One morning, I woke up pregnant. No idea how or when or even what had happened. I can't remember any of it. I hadn't even been out drinking." Then she added, "Might have been better if I had, but it was done, so no point worrying. I had to accept it. I suppose the only good thing was that I had no relatives to judge me. Well, apart from my sister, Harriet, of course. She just stuck her nose in the air and disowned me. Not a great loss, as she was never a particularly nice person. Anyway, a month later, I met George. We hit it off right away and were married within a couple of weeks. I have never regretted it," she finished firmly.

"Who are you talking to, love?" asked George sleepily.

"Just myself, George, just myself," she soothed. "You had better go home and get some sleep. I did mean to ask before you go. Did you remember to call your mum in Hawaii with the news?"

Millicent Daisy Weal was George's mother. She had moved to Hawaii with her American second husband shortly after meeting him while on holiday there. She had been worried about George's reaction to the news but he had been full of enthusiasm and encouragement. So she had departed, totally in love, for a little house just outside of Waikiki. Her happiness, unfortunately, was short-lived as her new husband died only three years after their marriage. But she loved Hawaii and chose to stay. Without fail, however, she phoned George and Marjorie once a week and sometimes twice a week since Marjorie's pregnancy.

"Oh God no, she will kill me," he replied. "I'd better get home and do that. I'll see you tomorrow." He bent over, kissed her, then Daisy, gave a quick wave and was gone.

For the next few days that Marjorie was required to stay in the hospital, George always came and spent a couple of hours with them, never missing an opportunity to pick up Daisy and drool over her. Marjorie was never sure whether

Daisy appreciated all the cooings and 'who's Daddie's liddle girl then', but she played along just fine, with large amounts of dribble and gurgling to keep him happy.

Finally, the day came when all the medical specialists, though still suspicious, could find no further excuse to keep them in the hospital and reluctantly agreed to allow them to go home the next day. George was visibly delighted.

He arrived bright and early the following day, happily wheeling a brightly decorated chair laden down with very bright pink baby clothes, pink toys and, perched on top, was a pink carrycot.

Oh God, thought Marjorie, who quietly hated pink; Daisy just giggled.

Chapter Two
Does Liquorice Grow on Trees?

Daisy was six months old when the first liquorice tree appeared. It must be said that Daisy did not yet understand that liquorice does not grow on trees but is, in fact, the root of a plant called 'Glycyrrhiza glabra', which is related to beans and peas. So we can, perhaps, forgive her as these events unfold.

George was quite partial to a bit of liquorice. In fact, he was a bit more than partial and, having run out, was suffering withdrawal symptoms. Marjorie didn't mind; at least he didn't smoke, so she didn't have to worry so much about any horrible diseases. It did make his teeth black though and she was forever reminding him to clean them before it became permanent, she joked. It also had the unfortunate ability of confining him, for extended periods, to the smallest room in the house. George, however, felt that his desire for liquorice outweighed all the disadvantages so he picked up the TV paper, determined that the match was not due to start for an hour and decided that he had time.

"I'll just pop down to the shop for some liquorice, love. I should be back in time for Mum's call," he told Marjorie.

"OK dear, get me some hard-boiled sweets. You know the kind I like. Never mind if you're late, I'll keep her talking until you get back," she replied, and then added, "Why don't you take Daisy with you?"

"Come on, Daisy," he said and to her absolute delight, swept her up into his arms, "we are going to the shop for some liquorice." He grinned at Marjorie. "And if we remember, some hard-boiled sweets for Mummy. None for you though; it's not good for new little teeth. I might buy you a peach if Mike's got any good ones."

Oh, he will have, thought Daisy, careful just to make pleasing noises and the occasional 'da da'. Peaches were her favourite, next to strawberries, of course, so she thought that the little dribble that her mouth involuntarily produced was acceptable.

George set off at a brisk gallop, because he knew that's what Daisy liked, bouncing her up and down as he went. Daisy, however, was using all of her self-control not to be sick. He skidded to a halt, much to her relief, outside Mike Madsen's Corner Shop, and then briskly reversed inside, pushing the door open with his back while holding Daisy to his chest.

"Hello George," said the small, wizened pair of eyes peering over the counter. "You know, I keep saying this, but I need a lower counter or longer legs." Not waiting for a comment, he continued, "Not watching the match, George?" It was more of a statement than a question, but Mike always managed to make both sound like accusations. In fact, anything Mike said sounded like an accusation, so people tended not to engage in too much conversation with him. Not that it mattered because Mike's conversations were always somewhat one-sided. He rarely noticed that people were talking to him. Though somehow, his brain managed to filter out requests for goods, which he collected and packaged on automatic while he continued to interrogate his customers.

"Well, I hope to be able to," he hinted, hoping Mike might speed up a bit. It was totally wasted, of course, because Mike didn't hear it anyway as he continued in his quest for information. "I'd like a nice peach for Daisy here," he continued. "A quarter pound of those," pointing to a jar of mixed sweets, "and half a pound of liquorice."

"You need to get up to date, George. It's grams now, not pounds." Again not waiting for a comment, he continued, "I haven't the time but it doesn't matter, it'll be repeated. Highlights on every news channel; comments everywhere; good film on later though; I expect you'll be watching that; GEORGE," he raised his voice, wrenching George back to the present, "you will be watching the film later, won't you?"

"Probably," George muttered as he grabbed his packages, paid his money and fled.

He did manage to get home in time to receive a roasting from Daisy's grandmother on the subject of liquorice, and how it was not good for you. He listened patiently and then said, "I love you too, Mum…talk to you tomorrow…bye," and very gently, replaced the receiver. "I love her dearly," he said to Marjorie, "but that woman will be the death of me."

"Now, now, George, be nice," said Marjorie.

Daisy thoroughly enjoyed her peach, ensuring that a liberal amount of juice managed to find its way into everything. It was hard being a baby especially dribbling on demand and carrying out all of the other unpleasant things that Marjorie had assured her were okay for a child her age. She did manage to warn Marjorie when they were alone of impending nappy disasters so that they could be avoided and the amount of bathing and washing reduced. But of course, when George was home, no such luxuries were possible.

George managed to watch his match and enjoyed his liquorice. He didn't watch the film, but instead had a thoroughly enjoyable evening playing with Daisy between the soaps that Marjorie insisted on watching.

That night from her cot, Daisy lay looking out at the back garden and an idea came to her. *Can I do it?* she asked herself and then giggled. *Mum says if you can't do it the first time, then keep on trying.* She concentrated, gathered her thoughts from all the far places of her mind, twisted them into the special shape needed and then…it was done. *I wonder what Dad will make of that.*

The following day, it was there and, to anyone who happened to see it, looking as if it had been there forever. Fortunately, it was in Daisy's back garden and not many people could see over the tall garden fence. George was extremely perplexed. He had never heard of such a thing. It hadn't even had time to grow. It was just there. I mean, come on, whoever had heard of a liquorice tree! It was impossible. It had to be a fake. It was someone's idea of a joke. So he pulled and prodded and examined from every angle, until finally he was forced to accept that it was genuine. Even though he was quite partial to a bit of liquorice, he could not quite bring himself to sample the tree's fruit. Odd-looking fruit it was too. Some were long and twisted, some were coiled up tight and some were straight and hollow.

George was a pragmatic sort of bloke, but this was proving too much.

"Marjorie!" he shouted. "Come quick!"

Marjorie came scurrying out of the house with Daisy clutched under her left arm in a decidedly undignified position and skidding to a halt, she pointed and said, "What's that?"

"I do believe it's a liquorice tree," observed George.

"Rubbish; impossible. Everyone knows liquorice is a root and doesn't grow on trees," declared Marjorie, and then leaning forward for a closer look, continued, "But I do believe you're right!" Her eyes shifted towards Daisy. "Now I wonder how that has happened? It really isn't something you see every day. Anyway, it came quick," her eyes were still looking at Daisy, "it will probably be gone tomorrow!"

I do believe that last bit sounded more like a command, Daisy thought. *I think she's onto me... Why didn't I know it doesn't grow on trees?*

"I've really got to go to the pub for a beer," said George.

"Far too early for the pub, dear," said Marjorie, "but we do have a couple in the fridge. I think I might join you."

"I suppose we ought to tell someone about this," observed George, "we could be famous. After all, it must be a world first."

Marjorie gazed at Daisy for a while before replying, "I don't think so, George, you've always said you would hate to be famous. You said you didn't have the temperament for constant interviews, photos and autograph hunters. Not to mention every gardener in the land on our doorstep, and all the government scientists wanting to dig up our garden."

"You are, as always, the practical one, my love," he said, "but just in case this is gone tomorrow, I think I shall get a bowl and pick some liquorice." His earlier fears disappearing with great speed as he looked at the abundance growing on the tree.

The following day, the tree was gone. George had enough liquorice to last for months so he was happy, but for some time afterwards, he could be found in the garden, gazing wistfully at the spot where it had been. Marjorie was relieved that the evidence had disappeared and awkward questions had been avoided. Daisy was pleased when the whole incident eventually faded from her parents' minds. She did notice her mother looking at her oddly from time to time, but the day that the first and only liquorice tree in the world had come to stay was soon forgotten and life, for a little while, returned to normal.

Chapter Three
Where Art Thou Milkman?

Daisy had reached two years old when the milkman disappeared. One second he was there, and the next he was gone. It was perhaps fortunate that it was early in the morning and no one was up to witness the miracle. He was only missed because one resident needed milk for breakfast and rang the dairy to find out where he was.

Gossip went up and down the street like wildfire, especially since his milk float had disappeared with him. There were rumours everywhere of various diabolical possibilities. He had been murdered and cut up, and had been spirited away by aliens, were two runners up. The favourite though was that he had run off with Suzy Flaunt from Povey Street. Poor old Suzy...well, not so old at only twenty-seven, had an unfortunate reputation and was frequently labelled 'flaunt by name, flaunt by nature'. So everyone was terribly disappointed when Suzy was spotted with a local plumber and they realised that running off would not have been very fast in a milk float anyway. So the favourite finally became 'spirited away by aliens'.

Police visited all of the houses on his route, asking questions such as, 'have you heard any weird noises' and 'have you seen any strange lights in the sky'. Then politely asking if they can 'search your garage please' as 'there may be clues you know'. Everyone knew that they were really only checking to see if you had hidden the milk float. Strangely, every time they appeared, Daisy was nowhere to be seen, but as soon as they had left, she reappeared bright and cheerful as usual.

Daisy noticed that her mother kept looking at her in an odd sort of way every time they were close and began to realise that Marjorie had been doing the 'odd look' thing quite often in recent times. So she tried to ignore it, until finally it was too much.

"He was fed up," she blurted.

"I thought it must be you."

"He wanted to, he really did."

"Daisy, no one wants to disappear. Now where has he gone?"

"Well, he did, he really did. I heard him say so," protested Daisy.

"Well! What pray, may I ask, did he have to say that he deserved to be turned into a disappearing trick?" It was a stern Marjorie so Daisy felt that honesty was becoming the safest policy.

"He said, 'I've really, really had enough of this. I'm fed up. I wish I was somewhere else.' I like him. He's nice, so I helped him along," defended Daisy.

"Where to?" persisted Marjorie.

"I sent him to one of the other places. He won't be lonely, he took his milk float with him," answered Daisy.

"What other places? What do you mean?" asked Marjorie.

"Oh, there are lots of other places," said Daisy, "In-between and outside. The outside ones are the worst. No one would like to go there. They sort of drag you into objects and you can't get out. So I sent him to an in-between one."

"Daisy, civilised people do not do things to people just because they ask. He didn't really mean it. Probably, he only felt a little down. Everyone does from time to time. It's part of life's... (*rich tapestry*, she was going to say, but it sounded stupid) part of life. You really should bring him back. I'm sure he'd rather be at home."

"What's a 'rich tapestry', Mum?"

From the surprised and indignant look on Marjorie's face, Daisy decided not to wait for a reply.

"OK Mum, but I have to wait for the right time. That'll be in the morning, I think."

●○●○●

Joe looked around at the landscape. He could see that its edges curved upwards into the distance and looked as if they would meet somewhere far overhead. The view was featureless, except for rolling grasslands, and dotted here and there were small trees laden with strange-looking, orange-coloured, tubular fruit.

It was light but he could not see any light source. He noticed that his milk float was here too, but it was like a cardboard cut-out with no thickness at all. So he decided to walk, only to find that he was not moving. His legs were, but he did not seem to be covering any ground.

He looked down at his feet and then at his legs, and twisting to see more, realised that he was flat too. He fought down rising panic, but then logic prevailed, *I'm thinking. I can see. I can move my bits. So flat can't be that bad*, he thought.

Luckily, Joe Drake was a good milkman but unlike the majority of his fellow workers, he was not particularly quick on the uptake, but his wife loved him and that was enough for Joe. If he had been a little brighter, his situation might probably have frightened him into a gibbering heap. But Joe was surprisingly calm. Much like a person who cannot really believe that what they are experiencing is real.

Out of the corner of his eye, he noticed a large insect hovering close to his head. But then as he concentrated on it, he saw that it was not an insect, but an arrow. Just like the curser on his computer. He reached up for it, touched it with a finger and it stuck. He moved his finger and the whole landscape shifted. Experimentally, he pointed at one of the little trees. Everything blurred as if his entire focus was on the tree. It rushed towards him and came to a stop with his finger just touching it. He pointed to another, then another, and another, each one flashing towards him to stop at his fingertip.

All this sudden movement makes me feel sick, he thought. *I gotta stop for a bit.*

Slowly, he pulled his finger away from the tree and with some relief noticed that the arrow stayed behind. He tried to sit down, but it appeared that bending was not an option no matter how hard he tried. He tried to turn around, but found that he could only twist his upper torso. He could feel the strain on his body increasing with each twist. So he stopped, fearful that being flat, he might tear himself. He reached towards the arrow and once again it stuck to his finger. He swept his arm from left to right, the landscape whirled before him and suddenly, he was facing the way he had come.

Far, far away in the distance, he could see his milk float and was shocked that he had come so far in such a short time. But was it a short time? It had been getting darker for some time, but it had only become apparent to him now as his attention was drawn to it. The more he concentrated on it, the faster the darkness came. It pushed in from all sides. It was a flat blackness that did not look at all nice. Quickly, he sought the familiar. He extended his arm and pointed into the distance. Again there was the queasy feeling, and he was standing next to the milk float.

He could hear sounds now, sliding sounds…slurping sounds…grinding sounds. He knew he was becoming frightened, but he didn't know why. He did not like the blackness or the sounds at all. He needed cover. He needed protection. *I wonder…could I?* he asked himself. Quickly, he pointed the arrow into the milk float's cab, and he was there inside. He was a flat person inside a flat milk float. Slowly, he withdrew his finger from the arrow. He felt the panic receding. Suddenly, he was so tired that his eyes closed and he drifted into sleep. Then the dreams came, of flat things that slid, slurped and grinded, of flat things with teeth that leapt out at him from the darkness. He screamed, but he couldn't wake up.

NOW, thought Daisy.

"Hello Daisy," said the milkman as he came through the front gate.

"Are your mum and dad OK...? How's your gran...? Lives in Hawaii or somewhere, doesn't she? Would you like to carry a bottle for me?"

He never offered the bottle though, so Daisy just trotted along behind him.

"Hello Joe, where you been?" she asked in her best two-year-old speak.

"Been? I haven't been anywhere, Daisy. What made you ask that?" asked a puzzled Joe.

"Nuthin'," muttered Daisy; *Good, he doesn't remember a thing.*

Joe set the milk on the front step, waved goodbye to Daisy, wandered off to complete his full round and went home. He had trouble with his wife who demanded to know where he had been and more importantly, who he had been with. He had even more trouble from the police who grilled him for hours and threatened him with prosecution for wasting police time. But worst of all, the dairy threatened him with the sack if such a thing ever happened again.

"I haven't bin nowhere," he kept insisting. "Is this some sort of joke?"

He was becoming convinced that either the whole world had gone mad or he had. They couldn't convince him that something had happened, and he couldn't convince them that it hadn't.

In the end, everyone had more important things to think about. Joe was popular so people easily forgot, things died down and it all went away. And the day that the milkman disappeared faded from the everyday mind, and into legend.

His friends, however, could never understand why Joe had suddenly developed an irrational fear of flat things.

Even a humble piece of paper would send him into a fit of trembling, which took hours to stop.

Chapter Four
The Hole That Jack Built

And then, Daisy was five years old. That's not to say that absolutely nothing of interest happened during those five years. But it would be true to say that nothing of significance did. She was at the stage where she could make her own calls to Grandma Millicent in Hawaii, without arousing suspicion. So every Wednesday she made her phone call and had to be dragged from the phone, where she would have been chatting all day given half a chance.

Daisy had learnt all of the lessons that a little girl needed to learn to survive her baby years. She learnt that some kids were nice and others were not. More importantly, she learnt that she had the ability to tell the difference. There was little Alfie from Oak Place just around the corner, who was really cute, but then there was Jack and James Swain from Ingle Road.

"Spawn of the Devil!" said Marjorie in one of her moments of more polite description.

"How can you say that, Mum?" asked Daisy. "They're only kids, same age as me."

"Spawn of the Devil," insisted Marjorie. "I have never come across two such evil kids. What surprises me," she continued, "is that the Swains are such lovely people. How they could have had two such horrible little monsters, as those two boys are, is beyond me."

"Can I go and play with Alfie, Mum?" asked Daisy.

"OK, but promise me that you will stay away from 'Grimly' and 'Fiendish'," said Marjorie.

"'Grimly' and 'Fiendish'?" queried Daisy.

"You know, Jack and James Swain," answered Marjorie.

"Oh no," grinned Daisy, waving as she ran to the front gate, "I like 'Grimly' and 'Fiendish' better."

"Be back at one for lunch," Marjorie shouted after her.

As Daisy made her way around the corner to Oak Place, she firmly settled herself into her five-year-old mindset. If you're a kid, you play as a kid. People just don't understand anything else. Oh, and don't forget, you use your hands to move stuff about and you have to climb on things the hard way.

Why can I do this stuff and nobody else can?

"*Stay a child for as long as you can. You'll learn soon enough,*" whispered a thought into her mind.

"*Who's that?*" shouted Daisy mentally. "*That wasn't me, who are you?*"

There was only silence, but Daisy knew beyond doubt that it was not her imagination and someone, or something, had spoken to her. She sent her thoughts outwards but could find nothing. So she drew back into herself with the determination that one day, one day, she would know.

She saw Alfie in the front garden of his house, chugging around on a toy tractor. Well, his feet were pushing the tractor along and his voice was doing the chugging, but who cares? To Alfie's way of thinking, he was driving a big John

Deere diesel tractor down furrows that were straight, clean and perfect. Daisy strengthened his thought and made him believe that it was a real John Deere before joining him, and then together they ploughed the field. The John Deere's diesel was as strong and as powerful as the sun that was shining down. The land was fertile and everything was as it should be. For just a little while, they were all grown up and their childhood forgotten.

Alfie never knew whether it was real or not when he was playing with Daisy, which is why he liked her so much. It seemed real but, of course, it couldn't be now, could it?

He had often asked, "Is this real, Daisy?" and she had always replied, "Do you want it to be?"

There was, however, a certain Jasper Reynolds who could never understand why his John Deere was always out of fuel and his fields were always ploughed. But being a pragmatic sort of man, he just thanked the Lord and gave money to charity.

"Alfie plays with g...irls, Alfie plays with g...irls," jerked them back to reality.

"What do you want?" Daisy asked Jack Swain, who was clambering over the front fence.

"Shut up, I don't speak to girls," he snapped.

"What you want, Jack?" asked Alfie. "Where is James?"

He whirled around as, "I'm behind you!" chanted James, who then promptly pushed him off of his tractor.

Daisy said nothing, but closed her eyes and reduced their shoes by one size. As with most children, parents tend to buy shoes a couple of sizes too big, to 'allow for growth', so nothing was immediately apparent. She reduced the shoes by one size again as Jack and James continued to push Alfie around, but nothing. So biting the bullet, she hit them with two size reductions. Both Jack and James were suddenly on the ground, howling and scrabbling at the Velcro fastenings on their trainers. Ripping off the shoes, they threw them away and fled, still howling, down Oak Place towards Ingle Road.

"What was all that about?" asked Alfie.

"No idea, but good riddance," replied Daisy, finding it difficult to hold back the laughter, but somehow she managed. As an afterthought, the discarded trainers returned to their original size. Just in case someone came looking for them.

"Someone really should do something about them," said Alfie.

"Oh! Someone will. I'm sure of it," Daisy replied, "but in the meantime, we have ploughing to do."

"OK, let's go." And so the morning went, ploughing the fields with the trusty John Deere, planting the crops, enjoying a ploughman's lunch and later bringing in the finest crop one's imagination could provide. And then it was over and it was lunch time.

"Bye Alfie, see you later," sang Daisy as she ran down the path to make her way home.

Later that day, Daisy thought that it was time for 'Someone' to surface. She really had no idea what 'Someone' was going to do, but she was determined that it would be spectacular and leave a permanent effect. Jack was the worst one and a really bad influence on James. James, however, was a willing pupil, so whatever lesson there was to learn, he had to learn it too.

Daisy crept out of the house and made her way to Ingle Road. Number twenty-two was the Swains' house and as she crept up, she could see both boys in the garden. Not much of a garden really. It was more holes than garden and it looked as if Mr Swain had given up filling them in after Jack and James who, at this moment, were enthusiastically adding a few more.

A really big hole, thought Daisy, *that's the answer*.

Making a quick mental check of the area, she reached out for the two boys. She lifted them, increasing their weight as they went. She wrapped them in a protecting field, muffling their squeals of fright. Up and up, she took them one…two…three hundred feet. At three hundred feet, they weighed upwards of half a ton each. She held them there while she concentrated her thoughts on the ground below. The garden, the lawn, all of its holes, shimmered and became black liquid, thick and sticky. Leaving on the protecting field, she released the two and then watched as they plummeted towards the ground. The impact was spectacular. Black goo hurtled up into the air in all directions. Acting as a shock absorber, it limited the depth of the hole to no more than twenty feet and about forty feet across. As the black goo poured back into the hole, they were carried upwards supported by the protecting field, until their heads were just above ground level. As the goo continued to fill the hole, pouring back from wherever it had landed as if it had a mind of its own, she released the protecting field. The goo lapped up around their necks, hardening as it came, then it shimmered and was normal lawn and garden again. That is, except for the two heads screaming, crying and bellowing from the middle of a lawn that had no holes and was perfectly manicured. Satisfied, Daisy went home.

Apparently, so her mum said the following day, Jack and James had been found buried up to their necks in the Swains' lawn. No one had any idea how it happened and the hysterical ranting of the two boys had not helped. It took more than four hours to carefully dig them out and as the future showed, they never dug a hole again.

Much later, Marjorie was heard to say: "You really could not get a better pair of boys than those that live at twenty-two Ingle Road."

Chapter Five
Does Being Green Help the Environment?

It was just before Daisy's sixth birthday and immediately after Grandma Millicent had rung to tell Daisy that a nice present was on its way to her, and that she hoped Daisy would have a nice birthday, when Jimmie D'Arco turned green and grew rather large yellow ears. That is not to say that it was permanent, but it did happen periodically. His mother despaired and his father, who was a doctor, seriously considered giving up the profession when it became apparent that a cure was not available on the National Health Service. But wait a minute, we haven't got there yet. Perhaps, I should start from the beginning.

As you have not met him yet, I will introduce Jimmie D'Arco. He is six years old, going on seven, and lives at sixteen Cross Street, which joins onto Ingle Road just near number forty-six. Jimmie is not a tidy, or particularly responsible, young man. True, he is polite but thoughtful and responsible, no. It could be said that his one saving grace was his friendship with a certain young lady named Daisy Weal.

They were inseparable, were Daisy, Alfie and Jimmie. It was about this time that Daisy and Alfie started to really notice their environment and as a result, they became collectors and disposers.

"Everywhere is so messy, Alfie," said Daisy.

"Never mind," said Alfie cheerfully, "we can collect up the rubbish and dispose of it."

So they collected and disposed, and it was only after a few days that they were noticed by a reporter from the local newspaper. Then there were the headlines, which screamed:

GREEN KIDS

Following up with a story that went on to say that children were never too young to be environmentally responsible, and here was a shining example to us all.

"Why do they call us 'green', Mum?" asked Daisy. "Nothing on me is green."

"It's a play on words," said Marjorie, "you see, most things natural and in nature are green. You know, green grass, green trees, that sort of thing. So they took the term 'green', and used it to describe anyone who is environmentally responsible. I don't take the view that all 'greens' are good for us. Some of them seem to have forgotten that we are part of the environment too."

"So I can take it as a compliment then?" queried Daisy.

"In this case, I think you can," replied Marjorie.

It was, however, some weeks before Daisy and Alfie realised that most of what they collected and disposed of, was deposited by Jimmie in the first place.

"Hey! Jimmie!" shouted Alfie one day. "You're depositing rubbish faster than we can collect it up."

"I pick up as well!" protested Jimmie.

"Yeh, but you just chuck it away somewhere else."

Jimmie looked confused.

"I didn't notice," he said. "It's all too much to think about when there is football and cricket and oh yes, athletics starts soon. Wait a minute, I like rugby too, and motor racing, especially the big motorbikes," he added.

"So do I," said Daisy, "but not all the time."

"But this is so boring," he protested.

And so it went, with Daisy and Alfie collecting and disposing carefully and Jimmie just disposing wherever he could, and protesting.

"I've had enough," he said one day, "I would rather turn green than keep on doing this. I'm going home."

He stomped off, muttering to himself. As he passed a bin, he reached in, pulled out a plastic coke bottle and threw it onto the grass verge.

"You keep on doing that, Jimmie D'Arco, and you will turn green," snapped Daisy, "and have long yellow ears," she added.

So there you have it. Every time Jimmie forgot and threw away anything, he turned green and sprouted long yellow ears. He only returned to normal if he retrieved the exact object that he had thrown away and disposed of it properly. It wasn't an easy transition, as Daisy had included a little pain to add to his discomfort. If you have seen the Incredible Hulk, then you will know exactly how it felt.

It was such an effective treatment that Daisy started to share it with other environmental assassins. The queues of green people with long yellow ears outside of all the surgeries in town had to be seen to be believed. The environmental agency and many, many specialists were called in from around the world, but no one could find a cure.

One day, a little girl came into the biggest meeting of the biggest minds and wandered up to the platform. Standing on a chair to reach the microphone, she said, "Hello."

Five hundred heads turned towards the platform and silence fell.

"The cure is simple," she said. "If you don't want to be green, be green and take your rubbish home." She stepped down from the platform, head held high, marched up the aisle and out of the door.

"Who was that?" someone asked.

"Dunno!" someone else said.

"Do you think she's got a point?" asked a third.

"Me, I'd try anything once," stated a fourth, rubbing his long yellow ears.

"Do you think taking any rubbish home would work, or do you think it has to be something that a person has specifically thrown away?" asked a woman, flicking her hair from her delicate green face.

Being very bright, in fact, the cream of the world's intellect, an agreement eventually emerged that the rubbish in question would have to be specific, and so a statement to that effect was issued.

Gradually, as if clutching at straws, the message slowly spread, gathering speed as it became obvious that the scientists were right. Some people, unfortunately, could not remember which piece of rubbish was to blame or where it had been left. So for a long time, rubbish tips were frequented by hundreds of green, long yellow-eared people sifting through them in an effort to find their offending piece of garbage. There was a portion of the population that returned to normal without retrieving their own rubbish, but the scientists finally concluded that this was due to the use of incinerators rather than landfill. And what happened to the town? Well, the town was the environmental envy of the world for many years. Oh, there was the occasional green person to be seen, but it was usually due to overwork, absentmindedness or the inability to locate their own special piece.

Jimmie? Well, it took a while before Jimmie seriously believed the message, but he did in the end. And sometime in the future, a certain Jimmy D'Arco goes into politics on an 'anti rubbish' ticket and eventually is appointed as Environmental Minister for the whole of the United Kingdom.

Chapter Six
Daisy and Her Namesake

Today was Daisy Weal's eighth birthday, and it should have been a great day. Grandma Millicent had been on the phone, singing 'Happy Birthday', without a lot of tune it must be said, and Daisy had opened her presents with less than her usual enthusiasm. Even so, it was a great day for Marjorie and George, and should have been for Daisy. But Daisy was not happy. The voice in her head was becoming more frequent. It was never informative, but only made comments. No matter how much she asked, explanations were never forthcoming. So, in the end, she had given up asking and just ignored it.

Tried to ignore it would be much more accurate. It is very difficult to do that when someone pops into your head without asking. So Daisy lived with her voice and lived with the fact that she had to be more, and more, careful, because the things she could do got bigger, and bigger, every day. She learnt quite quickly that she could not, under any circumstances, lose her temper. Particularly since the only time that this had happened, she had managed to break all the windows in the back of the house and flattened the whole of the backyard fence. It had been during the day when most people were either at work or out shopping, so she had quickly calmed down and managed to effect repairs without being seen. Well, she *had* been seen but only by old John who was still drunk from the previous night, when a well-meaning but misguided passer-by had given him an unwanted bottle of wine.

So it was for this reason that Daisy was not happy to be eight, and what didn't help was the fact that she was quite scared at what she might be able to do when she was nine.

"It's your day today, Daisy. What do you want to do?" asked George.

"Well, there is a Fair on in town. Can we go there?"

"Good idea," said Marjorie. "Then we could do the shops and have a birthday tea somewhere!"

"OK then," said George. "Everybody, get ready and I'll get the car."

A few minutes later:

"Can't get the car out, it's blocked in. Arthur's car on one side and Colin's on the other. Can't find either of them," complained George.

"Don't worry, Dad," said Daisy, "I'll go and find them."

Oh, of course, you haven't met Arthur and Colin yet, have you? Well, they live on either side of the Weals' house, Arthur to the right and Colin to the left. Arthur was Arthur Prentice who was an accountant for a small firm in town. Nothing spectacular, but reasonably well paid. Arthur was happy with his lot. He could provide for his wife and liked his job. He could even afford to have children, when his wife Monica could get her head around the idea. George liked him and they were good friends.

Colin was Colin Kilpatrick. Everyone called him 'Paddy' at his own insistence. He was a more private person at home, but was on 'over the fence' gossip terms with George. Colin had the broadest Northern Island accent that George had ever heard and George loved it.

"I could listen to Colin talking all day," he had often confided in Marjorie.

He was the Manager of the local village supermarket, and his customers loved him. His wife was Mary and as beautiful an Irish colleen as one could ever wish to meet. No children yet, but they were young and there was plenty of time.

Daisy ran around to both houses, but no one seemed to be in.

"Mr Kilpatrick, Mr Prentice!" she shouted, but there was no reply.

Oh well, here goes, she thought.

Doing a quick mental, 'security sweep' as she called it, she reached out using her thoughts and twisted them until they slipped into the required pattern. It was an easy thing to do and worryingly getting easier every day. The row of cars in front of George's slid forward ten feet.

Should be enough, she thought and ran back into her house.

"I found them," she lied, "and they've moved, so you can get out."

Marjorie looked at Daisy and raised an eyebrow.

"The cars around here are really, really quiet, don't you think?" she whispered as they followed George out of the house to the car.

Daisy Weal

They spent the morning at the fair, with George throwing balls at coconuts and Daisy directing the balls so that he actually hit them. After several goes, the stall holder asked politely if they would be kind enough to perhaps, "play on the dodgems" or perhaps "throw some hoops at the next stall".

They moved to the next stall and won so many goldfish that George had to give them back.

"I'm really good at this," he chuckled. "Let's go throw some darts, and then on to the dodgems."

"Yes dear," said Marjorie, looking at Daisy. "I really do believe that you are not good at darts. Isn't that true, Daisy?"

"Yes Mum," agreed Daisy, who was really good at taking hints, "but let him have a go. It should be fun to watch him miss anyway."

The darts stall was a total disaster, simply because George was actually not any good and with Daisy's mental assistance, he was even worse. Finally, he gave up and they wandered off to try the various rides. The merry-go-round, the big wheel, the octopus, the ghost train and the waltzer, on all of which Daisy resisted the temptation to interfere. But then they came to the dodgems.

"Come on, Daisy," said George, "you come on with me."

It was amazing. No one could hit them, no matter how hard they tried. George was just too elusive. Dodging and weaving, and boasting about how good he was. Time and time again, he took Daisy and then Marjorie, until they were both thoroughly fed up.

"I'll tell you what, Dad," said Daisy, "why don't you have one last go on your own?"

"OK," said George, "just you watch and learn."

It was a bigger disaster than the darts stall. Every car became a guided missile with George as the target. In the end, he staggered off, muttering about how he had lost the touch and was never going to ride a dodgem again.

Then they found a small tea shop in the centre of town, and it was cream cakes, ice cream and tea all around. Daisy opted for Pepsi Cola instead of tea. But nonetheless, it was probably…no, it was certainly the best birthday tea she had ever had.

"I'm stuffed," said George, "so let's pop over to yon antique shop," he pointed across the street, "and then go home."

Having all agreed enthusiastically, they made their way across the street to a small antique shop, quaintly called 'Old Antiques'.

"Aren't all antiques supposed to be old?" asked a puzzled Daisy.

"They sure are," agreed George, "but that's just a play on words. It's owned by a guy called Gary Old."

"Are you looking for anything particular, love?" asked Marjorie.

"Not really," said George, "I just want to mooch a bit."

So mooch they did, until George came upon one object, stopped and started to snigger.

"What's up, Dad?" asked Daisy, and then she noticed what he was looking at and continued, "What's that?"

"It's a printer," he said.

"No, it's not," said Daisy, "it's too big and clunky, and anyway, where do the ink cartridges go?"

"Yes," insisted George, "it really is. It's quite old. Even from before dot matrix printers."

He noticed her puzzled look and explained, "Dot matrix printers fired little rods against an ink ribbon to make dots on the page and if fired in the right sequence, then the dots would make up letters. Now this one uses a number of letters fixed on the end of spokes. As each one is needed, it revolves until it comes into contact with the ribbon. It is then pressed against the paper to make letters. It's that thing there." He pointed.

"Never heard of it," said Daisy, "what's it called?"

"It's named after you." Again he pointed, but this time at Daisy, and sniggered. Pausing for effect, he continued, "Well, because it's much older, I suppose it would be more accurate to say that you were named after it."

Daisy just looked puzzled. "Mum, I think Dad's lost the plot," she said.

"George, what are you babbling about?" asked Marjorie. "Stop confusing your daughter."

George just turned with a huge grin on his face and said, "I have not, my dears, lost the plot and I wouldn't dream of confusing anyone. However," he continued, hardly able to speak for giggling, "I have to inform you..." he paused to gather himself and wipe the tears of laughter from his face. "...That this is an IBM 'Daisy Wheel' printer."

Chapter Seven
A Postman's Holiday

Daisy was eight and a half years old when the postman went on holiday. That is, not to say that he actually chose his holiday or that he actually had decided to go on one. But as Daisy had rightly surmised, it had been a busy few months for him and he definitely looked very tired.

"Mum," she asked, "do you think Alfred...?"

Oh yes, you have met this one, but unfortunately, I neglected to tell you his name. His name is Alfred Correo. Correo in Spanish is pronounced Cor-ray-oh, and as coincidence would have it, means 'Mail' or 'Post'. He is, of course, of Spanish descent and had been the postman in Daisy's street for as long as she could remember.

"...needs a holiday," concluded Daisy.

"Don't we all?" said Marjorie, but being an experienced person in the field of one Miss Daisy Weal, she added, "But I'm sure he doesn't need any help. Anyway, I'm off to ring your grandma. Do you want to say anything?"

No, I don't suppose he does, Daisy thought, but aloud she said, "Yes, just say hi from me and I'll talk to her next week."

Perhaps I will send him to Spain for a couple of weeks...by the seaside... That's it. The sea air will do him good. Benidorm, that's a nice place, and he can visit his relatives.

So Benidorm it was. After all, Daisy was only a child of eight and she hadn't learnt that there were some things you didn't do and that there were times when interference was just that, interference.

●○●○●

"Arrg!" shouted Alfred as he materialised under the train engine on Benidorm beach. For those of you who have not been there, Benidorm beach has a number of poles in the sand with models of various kinds on them. A house, a train, a car, etc. It's an aid to people finding each other. "I'll meet you by the train," for instance.

"God, I hate sand. Grrr, and I hate water even more."

His materialisation had not had too much effect upon the existing holidaymakers who, for the most part, were made of sturdy stuff. Except that a circle of about twenty feet had cleared around him, just like water receding from a little higher ground. Wildly, he looked around and just across the road that bordered the beach, he spotted 'Jimmie's'.

From the wording that he could read at this distance, it looked as if 'Jimmie's' was an English place that served English food. He sensed a feeling of relief. At least he would be able to understand them. Alfred's ancestors had certainly been Spanish, but Alfred considered himself to be an Englishman. He had never bothered to learn Spanish and his parents had never insisted.

Daisy had done her work properly this time. That is to say, almost properly. The post office was in possession of an approved holiday application. Holiday pay had been moved into Alfred's bank account and sufficient money had been put into his pocket to cover immediate expenses.

After making enquiries to find out what sort of money he would need, Daisy had changed the money in his pocket into Euros. Having only ever seen Irish Euros that had been shown to her by Colin, that's what he got. She was so convinced that he would have a wonderful time that she never bothered to monitor him. She just set a retrieval time in her head and left it at that.

Alfred charged into Jimmie's. "Where am I?" he demanded.

"In Jimmie's," someone said helpfully.

"No, you idiot," screamed Alfred. "There's sea, and sand, and foreigners out there. What has happened to me?"

"Well, two things really," observed a heavily tattooed customer who seemed to be consuming a very large plate of sausage, egg and chips. "One, I think you have lost the plot. Two, you are apparently on holiday in Spain…in Benidorm to be exact. Three things actually," she glowered, "you are disturbing my lunch."

Alfred collapsed to the ground.

"How did I get here? I would never have booked this place. I hate the sea. I hate sand. I hate Spain. I want to go home." He was beginning to babble and the customers were starting to become concerned.

"Call the cops," someone suggested.

The guy behind the counter, having just replaced the telephone, returned. "Already have; the Guardia should be here soon."

The Guardia, or Guardia Civil to give them their proper name, are Spain's National Police Force. Towns have their own police force called 'Policia Local' or, in English, 'Local Police', who are responsible to the Town Hall, or *Ayuntimiento* in Spanish. But for serious problems, it's always the Guardia who are called.

Alfred had stopped babbling and started dribbling and blubbering, when the door swung open and two of Spain's finest, green-uniformed Guardia Civil Officers entered. Being totally unable to get any sense at all out of Alfred, they decided that custody was the best thing. Handcuffs were slapped on, Alfred was bundled into the waiting car and whisked away to a holding cell.

Having found no passport on him (that was Daisy's 'almost properly'), only Irish money and still not being able to get any sense out of him, the Guardia came to the conclusion that he must be one of those Irish terrorist people. Of course, we are aware that not all Irish people are terrorists. In fact, most are very nice people, but unfortunately, the Guardia were not so well informed and consequently, charged him under various terrorism acts.

A couple of days later, being in jail did not hold any delights for Alfred. The bed was awful, he was totally sick of *paella*, which was all they seemed to feed him, and the Spanish coffee had left his tongue raw. Then the door opened and he was escorted into court before a Spanish judge who looked suspiciously like a bandit out of the movies. As no one could understand the other, he was sentenced to a fine of all the money he had and immediate deportation back to Ireland.

On arrival in Dublin, he was immediately arrested for having no passport and being penniless. He was thrown into an Irish jail, 'while enquiries are made' and then seemingly forgotten.

After about eight days in an Irish prison, being in jail still did not hold any delights for Alfred. The bed was awful, Guinness was beginning to make him ill and he was totally sick of soda bread and potato bread, which was all they seemed to feed him. He was looking forward to being able to explain and plead with an Irish judge. He was sure he could make him understand.

The door opened and he was escorted into court before an Irish Judge who straightened her wig and glared at him. For Alfred, that was the low point. He did manage to convince her that he was English and was relieved when he was sentenced to be deported to England without delay.

On arrival at Heathrow, he was immediately arrested for having no passport and being penniless. He was thrown into jail, 'while enquiries are made'.

A couple of days later, his identity confirmed, he was released under caution and sent home. Or rather, he was shoved out of the door with no money to somehow get home by himself. After about five hours of hitchhiking, he arrived home to a wife and children who totally ignored him and refused even to acknowledge his presence. As Alfred tended to be a bit wicked at times, he thought, *in all black clouds, there is a silver lining*, and immediately went to bed.

The following day, he went to the post office and found that he still had about two days of holiday left. Having had more than his fill of holiday, he managed to persuade his boss to let him return to work and recommence his rounds.

●○●○●

"Hello Daisy," said the postman as he passed her gate.

"Hey," said Daisy, "wait a minute; you are supposed to be in Spain on holiday. You aren't due back yet."

The postman turned and stopped in surprise for a moment.

"Now how would you know that, young lady?" he asked. "…No matter," he continued, "after that really odd experience, the only holiday I'll ever need in the future is a Busman's Holiday."

"What's a Busman's Holiday?" she asked.

"It's a holiday where you do what you always do. In my case, that's delivering letters. And if anyone even remotely suggests another holiday abroad or anything that does not involve the Royal Mail, I think I may commit murder."

"They're likely to arrest you for that," said Daisy thoughtfully.

"It's only a figure of speech, Daisy, I don't think I would really kill anyone. Well, probably not anyway. I've seen enough of the inside of prisons to last me a lifetime."

"OK, Mr Correo," said Daisy meekly.

As he walked away, however, he was more than a little puzzled by the fact that she had added, "I'll remember that for next time."

Chapter Eight
Odd Things Happen in Brighton

A couple of weeks later, and only a smidgen over eight and a half years old, Daisy was into geography in a big way. Mainly because this term it was about England and she had found that she liked England a lot. You could say that our Daisy was becoming a very patriotic young lady indeed. During the lesson, though no one believed him, the teacher had insisted that there *were* people who actually went to Brighton.

Daisy was eight…well OK, eight and a half. She may have a sophisticated mind whose origin was as yet unknown, but nonetheless she was in actual fact still only eight (and a half). She had the same irresponsible streak as all eight-year-olds and was just as mischievous. She managed to control most of her urges most of the time, but there were still times when people reached for things and those things just slipped out of reach at the last moment. Shoes came undone at inopportune moments and skirts, trousers and knickers fell down without warning. Occasionally, car doors became welded shut, but in Daisy's defence, she had never done that while the car was occupied.

But these were little things, and the urge was becoming stronger and stronger with every passing moment to do something very large and very spectacular. It was becoming too much for Daisy to handle alone, so after a massive inward struggle, she decided to confide in her mother.

"I need to talk, Mum," she said, "it's important."

"OK dear," said Marjorie, a little taken aback by the serious look on Daisy's face, "fire away. I'm listening."

So she told her mother everything. All of the things she had done and about the voice in her head and finally, about the things that she wanted to do. It took an hour, and even then she only stopped when her breath ran out and sat waiting patiently for the verdict.

Marjorie sat silently for a while and then reached out and took Daisy's hands.

"I knew you could do things, but I didn't realise how powerful you really were. Though I bet Jasper Reynolds misses his fields being ploughed now that you are too big for the tractor." Then she became serious. "I am relieved that, at your age, you've managed to show such self-restraint. I'm also relieved that you felt able to confide in me. Lastly, I'm relieved that you have this voice in your head that seems to stop you when you need to be stopped." She paused. "I don't pretend to know what is happening here, and I don't pretend that I have all the answers, but I do know that for such pressure to go untapped can only be dangerous for you and for everyone around you. You must find an outlet. Something you can do that won't harm people." She paused again. "The good thing, I suppose, is that if you were to slap St Paul's Cathedral on the Moon, you could do so without any damage to it and return it in the same way."

"Actually," said Daisy, "I'm not sure that I could, with such an old stone-built building. So I don't think I'll try that one—" She stopped, then winked and said, "Maybe…one day…you never know."

"Just be careful, Daisy," warned Marjorie. "Anything major, please come to me first."

"I will, Mum," she said, "I promise."

Daisy grew that day, not in age, but in stature and maturity. The world did not know it and probably never would, but that simple conversation had probably saved it from some spectacular disasters.

"*You did it right, now practice control,*" said the voice in her head.

For the first time, Daisy accepted the advice without animosity or anger, and thought, "*I will, I will, but what I need is a really long trip.*" Her thoughts paused. "*I know, the Moon.*"

"*Bit ambitious, don't you think?*" the voice asked.

"*I have to try sometime. I'll build in a failsafe to kick me back here if anything goes wrong, and I'll make sure I take enough air.*"

"*Good girl. Go for it.*"

Daisy realised that for the first time, she was actually having a conversation with the voice, so she asked, "*What can I call you?*"

"*Our real name is Vanaelcrocedus, but you can call us **Vana**.*"

"*Thank you. Now I think is the time to go. First though I have to tell Mum, because I promised.*"

She looked up and noticed that her mother was looking at her with a question in her eyes. She realised that she must have looked odd while she was silently having a conversation with the **Vana**.

"It's decided, Mum," she said. "I'm going to make a try for the Moon. *Vana* thinks I'm ready."

"*Vana*?" queried Marjorie, then she realised. "Oh, I see, the voice now has a name." She paused. "Be careful, Daisy, be careful."

All the thoughts and all the power started to slip into place, twisting and turning, to find the right pattern. She could feel the *Vana* guiding and reinforcing. She surrounded herself in her protecting field, made it airtight and launched. Marjorie, despite expecting something, jumped as there was a sharp popping sound, a sudden waft of wind and Daisy disappeared.

A tiny eight-year-old girl suddenly materialised in the centre of the Sea of Tranquillity. Flickered once, twice, three times, and then vanished, and she was back at home with her mother.

"*Brilliant*," thought the *Vana*. "*Try again.*"

Marjorie jumped again as Daisy reappeared. "That was quick," she said.

"Sorry Mum, almost but not quite…trying again."

Once again, she gathered her strength, following the path that the *Vana* had shown her. Twisting her thoughts into the pattern, she held it and launched.

She was there, in the Sea of Tranquillity. A little insubstantial at first, and flickering, but after a few seconds she settled and was there in full. She looked around in awe and gazed at the rim of the crater in the distance. She felt incredibly light and did an experimental hop, soaring four to six feet above the surface.

This is great, she thought, *what I need is a house here.*

For nearly an hour she jumped and soared in gravity no more than one sixth of the Earth. She ran in enormous leaps, somersaulting and dancing as she went, until finally, spent and exhausted, she sighed, *That's enough for now, and it must be nearly tea time. So I'd better get home; Mum will be worried.* To be on the safe side, she kicked in her failsafe and was there, at home, in the kitchen, in front of an obviously relieved Marjorie.

After tea, Daisy went to her room to practice. She picked Brighton because it was the subject of a lesson at school. First, she moved her mind there and after a moment, her mind made up, she moved the sea eight miles away from the beach. She did make sure that it was only water and fish and not people that moved. It was actually quite amusing to see people suddenly finding themselves swimming on the sand. Then she let it flow back, but only slowly, like a tide coming in.

She turned her attention to the pier and gradually, it started to turn until she had made a question mark out of it. Then she continued to turn it until both ends were on the beach and only the middle was out to sea. That was the most difficult part because she had to make all the materials that it was made of bendy, and flexible. By this time, hysteria had gripped the beach, the pier and the hotels opposite. But Daisy was careful. She reached out and protected anyone in danger, cradling them and moving them to safety. She released her hold on the pier for a few moments and then started, inch by inch, to move it back into its original position. It was tiring, but she persisted until it was completely restored.

Now that she knew she could manipulate large objects, she started scanning around for a suitable building. As soon as she saw it, she fell in love. This was it. It looked like a castle, all towers, battlements and even Minarets.

This was the place, and a trip into a local mind told her what it was...this was the Brighton Pavilion. She gathered it up right down to its foundations. Any people that were in it she carefully moved out, and then going far back into her own mind, she gathered her power, concentrated, twisted reality and launched.

No one knows yet, but the Brighton Pavilion sits, in all of its glory, in the middle of the Sea of Tranquillity on the Moon. Daisy had made sure that the foundations were intact, and sank them into the Moon's surface with exactly the same support as they had had before. She moved the air with it and surrounded it in a retaining field to make sure that there was no atmosphere loss. Then she moved away from it and stood back to admire her efforts. *It's perfect*, she thought, *no one could wish for a better home on the moon than that*.

She finally realised that she was calm and at ease. All of her tensions were gone, so she returned to her body, serene in the knowledge that she could do great and amazing things. Along with that realisation came the sure and certain knowledge that she was not God and could control herself with a degree of responsibility that she had not been sure that she possessed. The thought that perhaps stealing the Brighton Pavilion was not entirely responsible did cross her mind. But it was satisfying though and it could always be put back now, couldn't it?

Various headlines adorned the papers over the next few days. Firstly, about the odd low tide that had occurred, and then about the impossible antics of the pier, which no one believed, and then finally, about the disappearance of the Brighton Pavilion. But of them all, Daisy's favourite was: ODD THINGS HAPPEN IN BRIGHTON.

Chapter Nine
Is the Moon a Nice Place to Live?

Two months before her ninth birthday, Daisy was spending a few idle hours watching the television, when it was interrupted for coverage of the NASA mission to the moon. It was well over 40 years since the last one in 1969, so there was a lot of interest and hours of coverage on the media.

"Mum!" screamed Daisy in panic. "It says they're going to the Sea of Tranquillity."

"Yes dear!" said Marjorie.

"But they can't, they really can't," wailed Daisy.

"Why not?" asked Marjorie. "If you're going to the moon, it seems entirely reasonable."

"They can't, because that's where I put the Brighton Pavilion."

"Oh my God!" said Marjorie. "What did you do that for?"

"I needed somewhere to stay while I am on the Moon. It's big, holds loads of air and it looks really nice where it is."

Marjorie raised her eyebrows. "You go…and stay…the Moon?"

"Yes, of course," answered Daisy, "it's really nice. Would you like to come?"

So that's where she keeps disappearing to, thought Marjorie, *my very own eight, going on nine, year-old astronaut.*

"That is a very nice offer, Daisy," hesitated Marjorie, "but I think…well, I think…no, if that's alright with you?"

Daisy looked thoughtful for a moment and then suggested, "I could make them land somewhere else."

"No," insisted Marjorie. "It's too dangerous. You would be gambling with people's lives."

"Alright then," said Daisy, "I will just have to go and greet them when they arrive."

"Yes dear," said Marjorie and thought, *and that will be a seriously interesting sight indeed.*

○○○○○

"Houston, this is the Luna Module initiating burn for separation."

"Burn for separation…confirmed."

"Commencing rotation for braking manoeuvre."

"Rotation…confirmed."

"Commencing burn for deceleration."

"Burn for deceleration…confirmed."

"Descent to the Sea of Tranquillity commenced."

"Descent…confirmed."

"Houston, this is the Luna module. There is a large area of sunlight reflection down there."

"Please repeat, Luna module."

I'm fed up with this rubbish, thought Chuck Landers.

"No, you heard me the first time and anyway, you can replay the recording, and if you say 'confirmed' one more time, I shall scream."

"Con… OK."

"We'll get a better look when we land. I'll let you know if it's anything then."

"Affirmative, Luna module."

"That's worse!" grumbled Chuck. "What exactly is wrong with, 'OK Chuck'?"

Silence greeted him and he returned his attention to the serious business of bringing the lander down in one piece.

The Luna Module eased itself down onto the Moon's surface, its engines throwing up huge amounts of dust that very slowly drifted down to settle after the massive thrust died away.

"Excuse me, Chuck," said Nate Connors, "it's a long way away, but I do believe there's a building over there!"

"He's right, you know," said Brett Chase, who was the third person in the cabin, "funny thing is, I recognise it. But how can it be true? I reckon that we're all hallucinating."

He rubbed his eyes and looked again. "Nope, it's still there. You know, I've got relatives in England; well, they sent me this newspaper with an article about strange goings on in a town called Brighton. There was this big buildin' that disappeared, called the Brighton Pavilion. Well, they had a photo of it, and that," he said, pointing, "looks just like it."

"Stop messin' with me," said Chuck as he leaned over to look. He stopped, rubbed condensation off the Plexiglas and looked again.

"Oh God, you're right," he said. "Why do things like this happen on my watch? What are we going to tell Houston?"

"What do you mean 'we'?" asked two voices in unison.

"If you think that I am going to do this alone, you guys are sadly mistaken. For now, I'm saying nothing. Let's suit up and go for a walk."

Thirty minutes later, all landing checks complete, helmets on, visors firmly closed, they cracked the hatch and jumped in slow motion into the dust below. Chuck was first, as was his privilege as commander of the mission. But he had hardly touched the ground before he was followed closely by Nate and Brett.

"Hello," said Daisy, coming around the lander, "do you like my house?"

"Argg," spluttered Nate, who was the first to notice her, leaping about twenty feet away in his panic, "what's that?"

Now Chuck was Commander and he had been trained for difficult and unusual situations, but this really was outside of his field of experience.

"N-n-n-not quite s-s-s-sure," he stuttered. "I think it's a little girl, and I think she's trying to talk to us. Well, her lips are moving anyway."

"I have two questions really," said Brett very calmly. "How did she get here, and why ain't she dead?"

"*Daisy,*" thought the ***Vana***, "*they can't hear you. They are all sealed up inside those suits. You'll have to speak to their minds.*"

"*Of course,*" returned Daisy, "*and sound can't travel where there's no air, can it?*"

She turned her attention to the astronauts and projected her thoughts towards them.

"Sorry, forgot where I was for a moment. I said 'Hello, do you like my house?'. Just think your answer. I will hear it."

"Th-th-that's the Brighton Pavilion from England, isn't it?" faltered Brett, still speaking aloud.

"*Yes,*" thought Daisy, "*looks really nice there, doesn't it?*"

The astronauts had started to walk towards the Pavilion, and Daisy skipped along to keep up. Massive big skips they were as well.

"You are not real," stated Chuck,

"*Yes, I am,*" thought Daisy, "*at least my mum thinks so.*"

"*Would you like to come in for tea?*" she continued. "*It will be really nice. The Moon is a nice place to live, don't you think?*"

She realised that must have been the last straw, for she was alone, and they were racing, in great big leaps, back towards the lander.

For a little girl, it is always difficult to judge the passage of time, but it seemed like only seconds before the lander's engines belched fire and it leapt in a great cloud of dust into the sky and was gone.

"Must have been something I said," she murmured aloud.

Chapter Ten
Some Things Are Best Forgotten

Almost a full day had passed and it was not immediately apparent but the returning Moon mission was in trouble. All systems 'nominal' was reported to NASA by a slightly hysterical crew, but trouble was brewing and no one knew it yet.

The three astronauts were still recovering from the spectacle of a very lively eight-year-old galloping about the moon and had not come to terms with it yet or even agreed what they would report. What made it even worse was that 'it' had invited them into the Brighton Pavilion, on the Sea of Tranquillity, for tea. They hadn't accepted, of course. They were too busy fleeing towards the landing module, with the serious intention of leaving as quickly as possible.

Mission Control at Houston had given up trying to find out why the mission had been abandoned so abruptly and just concentrated on the job of bringing them home safely. There would be time later for recriminations and interrogations. It was becoming apparent though that these three were unstable and extra care would need to be taken in dealing with them.

Out of the depths of space and across time, '***Something***' was coming. Unseen and unheard, but coming nevertheless. To all intents and purposes, it took no time at all, but the distances involved were so great that some time had actually passed before they found themselves gazing down upon the small blue ball that was Earth. They had been drawn to this place. The ***Vana*** was here, and they had somehow missed it. Normally, wherever part of the ***Vana*** was, then so were they. The universe had given birth to them both at the beginning of time and the only mission that they had ever had, or more accurately knew they had, was to frustrate the efforts of the ***Vana***. It was only part of the ***Somethings*** that was here. They were not individuals, but part of what you could call a 'hive' mind, who just sent bits of itself to wherever they were needed.

The ***Somethings*** were similar to the ***Vana***, who were also a 'hive' mind, but they did differ from them in a one fundamental way. Where the ***Vana*** had immense power and the ability to move galaxies, the ***Somethings*** could only operate on small things, tiny things, irritating things...but...they were so many that they did not miss very much. They had one advantage and this was the fact that the ***Vana*** were not aware of their existence. For when you are able to move an elephant with your mind alone, why would you notice an ant that somehow got moved with it?

●○●○●

Daisy was in her favourite place in the garden, sitting cross-legged in the sand pit. Here, she could set her body to automatically play in the sand while her very active mind soared to wherever she wanted to go. But today, she was just practising small things and enjoying the summer sun.

Suddenly, she became still. "***Vana***," she said aloud, "something has arrived. Something is out there!"

"*We don't sense anything, Daisy. It must be your imagination.*"

"No, it's not," insisted Daisy, "see into my mind. See what I see."

The ***Somethings*** recoiled in horror when it realised that here was part of a ***Vana*** that could sense its presence. Then it noticed that the ***Vana*** was being carried on another mind, a small and much less powerful mind. It was that mind that had found it.

"*Who are you?*" demanded the ***Vana***. "*And why are you here?*"

"*Who?*" came the reply. "*Who? We are what we are, and we are here because you are.*"

"*Why?*" asked the ***Vana***.

"Apparently," came the quiet reply, "*you were created with no limits, and became so powerful that something was required to keep you in check.*" A moment passed. "*Something to stop you thinking you were God. So along we came with the task of frustrating your efforts. There is nothing like a small irritating mistake, something you think you have failed to consider, that is better designed to bring you down to Earth, so to speak.*"

It seemed to be learning quickly, and continued, "*Wouldn't have worked if you had known we existed. We are not evil, and in most things, we are not deliberate. Our actions seem to be more like instinct. We can't help it. It just happens. There is one snag though."*

"What's the snag then?" asked Daisy.

*"If we are somewhere, and even if the **Vana** is not there anymore, we still do things. Sometimes the things we do have fatal consequences, and for this we are sorry but, as I have said, we have no control and mostly…"* The **Somethings** paused, and Daisy detected amusement. *"…we just play practical jokes."*

Oh God, thought Daisy, *an entity older than time, and it plays practical jokes*. Directing her thoughts, she continued, *"How come it's taken both of you so long to notice this place?"*

They didn't answer the question, and Daisy got the distinct feeling that she probably would never be given the answer either.

"As we have said, sometimes we are sorry for what we do, but we can't help it and nothing can usually be done to correct it. We discovered a space vehicle as we were coming. It was different to those we have seen before, and we interfered. If you can, you must do something, for it's now in serious trouble and it's our fault."

●●●●●

A few thousand miles above the Earth's surface and still in the darkness of Space, the Space Shuttle was manoeuvring into position for insertion into its approach window.

The approach window is the angle that they must come in at so that they don't bounce off the Earth's atmosphere. Chuck, Nate and Brett were fully suited with face plates open, frantically doing the things that astronauts do to keep themselves alive.

Outside and all around them, recently arrived ***Somethings*** were hard at work, and gradually the adhesive that bonded the ceramic tiles of the heat-shield to the underside of the Shuttle began to break down. Ceramic tiles are used because they are heat-proof, and as the shuttle enters the atmosphere, the friction against the air makes it get very hot indeed. Without the heat shield, the shuttle would burn up in seconds.

"Houston, we are in the 'window', and atmosphere contact should be in about 30 seconds."

"Ok Chuck, got that."

Well, at least I've got rid of the confirmed and the affirmatives, thought Chuck.

The Shuttle hit the edge of the atmosphere. It was going so fast that the air around it became super-heated with friction. The weakened adhesive could no longer hold the tiles of the heat shield and they began to peel off. Without the heat shield to protect it, the skin of the Shuttle began to glow. The Astronauts had only seconds to live.

Daisy appeared in the cabin.

"Don't ask," she said. "We have to go, and we have to go now."

She gathered them to her and, with the ***Vana's*** help, she launched.

Chuck, Nate and Brett found themselves in the middle of the runway at Edward's Air Force base, gazing up at a spark as it streaked across the sky. A spark that became ten, and then a hundred, expanding as it went, becoming brighter and brighter, before suddenly fading and was gone.

"Well!" said Brett. "I really, really do believe that, that is something best forgotten."

"So do I," said Chuck, and started heading towards the buildings in the distance. "Come on. Let's see if we can convince them that we chickened out and didn't go at all."

●○●○●

"You will be glad to know," the ***Somethings*** said as Daisy reappeared in the sandpit, "that even if the ***Vana*** leaves, we will remain. We have convinced *Coincidence* that it has no place here and we will take care of everything from now on."

"I didn't know that *Coincidence* could be convinced of anything, I just thought it happened," said Daisy.

"*Oh no,*" the ***Somethings*** said. "*It's something like us, but there are not as many of them.*"

The ***Somethings*** knew that now the rules had changed, and that the ***Vana*** were at last aware of their presence. How that would affect the Universe, only time would tell.

Oh dear, thought Daisy, *but at least I will know who to blame when I trip over my laces, or if my elastic breaks and my knickers fall down. I'll know which **something** has caused it.*

Chapter Eleven
Aunt Harriet

Daisy's ninth birthday was next week and as we are well aware, the passage of birthdays is not something that filled her with delight. In fact, she approached them with caution and a lot of worry. She was alone inside her head now. The *Vana* had left, saying that she did not need them for the time being. Just like that…poof…gone.

Apparently, the newspapers had said in the beginning that the Moon mission had been a con perpetrated by three NASA astronauts. They went on to say that those same three astronauts had been detained under some obscure Mental Health Act, and locked away in a centre for the criminally insane. There they would have stayed, if it had not been for a Russian orbital vehicle that photographed, in stunning colour and pin-sharp imagery, the Brighton Pavilion as it passed over the Sea of Tranquillity.

Would that be enough to release them? Well, not really. The key, however, was in the close-ups that revealed something tiny, with two arms and two legs, waving at the vehicle as it passed overhead. Then they were released and various newspapers paid huge sums in compensation and then further huge sums for their stories. Eventually, it all died away with the three astronauts retiring to the country in an attempt to forget the whole thing altogether.

●◐●◑●

A nut had fallen off her bike that morning, making her saddle suddenly drop down. Daisy was not amused.

"**Somethings**," she said out loud, "you are messing with me. Keep on going, and I will turn you all into soup."

"*Err sorry, but it is habit.*"

"Well, don't do it again," snapped Daisy.

"*We'll try.*" Again, there was amusement. "*But we can't promise anything.*"

So Daisy pushed her bike home for her dad to fix, only to find herself greeted by an excited Marjorie.

"My sister is coming for your birthday," she blurted.

"Sister? What sister?" demanded Daisy, who then gabbled, her words tumbling together, "I didn't know you had a sister. You never told me you had a sister. Does that mean that I've got an Auntie? Who is she? Where is she coming from?"

Aunt Harriet was Harriet Annabelle Carsons. She was married to Robert Carsons who was an English Structural Engineer who, being very good at his job, had been offered a well-paid position in Canada. He had promptly accepted, and they had immediately moved there. Aunt Harriet was not a nice lady, not a nice lady at all, but she had finally been overwhelmed by conscience and thought that it was her duty to forgive her little sister. Besides which, she was also curious to see this fatherless whelp that was her niece.

"Yes dear, but I did actually mention her just after you were born. She's your Aunt Harriet, and she's coming home from Canada for a short visit. We lost touch,"—she shrugged her shoulders—"don't know why really. It didn't make much sense to tell you when I thought you would never meet her."

"She should be here about three days before your birthday," she continued. "Oh, and Daisy, please try to be just human for the few days she's here."

"But I am human," protested Daisy.

"You know what I mean. Please do not manipulate her chemistry in any way whatsoever, and above all, be nice."

"I am always nice, and I promise I won't manipulate, whatever that is, anything." As an afterthought, she added, "Can't make promises for the somethings though."

"What?" asked Marjorie. "What somethings? What do you mean?"

"Oh, nothing really, Mum," replied Daisy.

Marjorie thought it best not to press the matter as she was sure that she probably could not cope with the answer. So instead, she changed the subject. "What's up with your bike anyway, and why have you pushed it home? Couldn't you have fixed it, like…thought…at it or something?"

"Something," said Daisy, though her mother missed the use of the word as a name, "something nicked the saddle nut. I suppose I could have fixed it, but what use are dads if they don't get to fix things for their kids?"

"True," agreed Marjorie, "very true."

The next few days seemed to fly by, with Daisy getting more excited by the minute as she let her imagination run wild thinking of her brand-new Aunt Harriet. She would be tall and very beautiful, love her new niece to bits and be lots of fun to be with.

Finally, the day arrived and there coming through the front gate was Aunt Harriet, stunningly beautiful, slim and very tall.

"Hello Harriet," said Marjorie, "long time no see."

"You really aren't looking too bright, Marjorie," said Harriet, and then looking at Daisy, "And I suppose this is the brat? Quaint little house you have here. Not sure how I'll feel in such a small place. Not really got much garden either, have we? Not really what I am used to at all. No, not at all."

Daisy stood looking at her, trying very hard to smooth the distaste from her face.

"Are you sure, Mum," she asked finally, "that I am really, really not allowed to manipulate anything?"

"There is a distinct possibility that I may have been hasty, Daisy. Let's wait to see what the next few days bring."

"Can't imagine what you two are babbling about," said Harriet, breezing past them into the house. "Wallpaper looks a bit tired. Place could do with a lick of paint. I have always thought that George wasn't of much use."

"I notice you haven't brought Robert with you," Marjorie retorted. "Afraid he might embarrass you?"

Oh dear, thought Daisy, *this is going to be quite an interesting few days.*

"I had forgotten how nice she was," confided Marjorie sarcastically to Daisy, after Harriet had been there for a few days, constantly sniping at everything.

Today was Daisy's ninth birthday, and the only thing missing was a card, or present of any kind, from Aunt Harriet. "Don't believe in them. Unnecessary expense," was all she had said.

"Do you know," Marjorie continued indignantly, "this morning, she even told me my knickers were the wrong colour."

"I did know where she was," she confessed, "and I didn't contact her because I was afraid she would be like this. When she said she was coming over, I suppose I hoped—"

Suddenly, there was an ear-splitting scream from the house.

"I think," said Daisy, "that she may have discovered the zit, and the slight yellowing of the teeth. Oh, and the fact that she's put on a few pounds and has suddenly developed a slight stoop. I really am sorry, Mum, but I think 'manipulation' might be my middle name." She looked at her mother and added, "What do you think of, perhaps, a squint tomorrow, and could I give her dandruff?"

"Whatever would I do without you, Daisy?" said Marjorie, smiling broadly. "Whatever you like." But she added as an afterthought, "Please don't make it permanent. After all, she is my sister and even if she is horrible, I still love her."

So it came to pass that Aunt Harriet blamed Marjorie for all her woes and decided to return to Canada early. A tall, beautiful and incredibly graceful Aunt Harriet had arrived for Daisy's birthday, and a small, wizened, ugly, stooped hag of an Aunt Harriet, with teeth that would do justice to a banana, left.

Daisy had decided to explain to Marjorie about the **Somethings** and about the fact that they had replaced *Coin-*

cidence as everyone's daily irritant. So she was able to tell her mother that she had persuaded a few...well, a couple of thousand really, to go and spend a year or so with Aunt Harriet.

"It will gradually wear off over about a year," she explained. "I can't, however, be so sure about the ***Somethings*** leaving. You never know, they might like it there."

Aunt Harriet arrived at Toronto International Airport, and was immediately arrested on suspicion of being an illegal immigrant using someone else's passport. As she was such an unpleasant individual and shouted at the Customs officers, she was strip searched and thrown into a holding cell. Harriet used her phone call to telephone Marjorie for help, but as Marjorie quite rightly pointed out, it was not her place to interfere in Canadian justice. Apparently, for some reason, Harriet's husband Robert felt the same way too.

It took several months for Harriet to work her way through the Canadian legal system, before being found guilty and sentenced to deportation. It seemed though that this could only happen if the authorities could ever find out what nationality she was. She was interviewed by virtually every consulate in the country, but not one of them was prepared to accept responsibility. So she stayed, for the time being, in jail.

Chapter Twelve
Burglars and Trendal Place

Daisy was nine but she, like all children of her age, counted age with a considerable degree of accuracy. So she was really nine years, two weeks and one day old when the burglars came to Trendal Place. As you know all too well, number twelve, Trendal Place, is where Daisy lives, in a pretty little double-fronted detached house with a small but adequate garden and, for George, a perfectly sized garage.

So therefore, we are safe in our assumption that one pair of sneaky burglars had made a serious error of judgement when they picked this place for their illegal activities. They were, in a way, helped by the fact that they did not specifically target Daisy's house and as a result were saved from the full extent of her wrath.

Daisy had just returned from a trip to the USA, having enjoyed visiting a very remote area of the countryside where a certain Mr Chuck Landers lived. He had started to enjoy her visits to his small ranch, after recovering from the shock of the first one, and she enjoyed his company and his horses, especially his horses. He still refused to accept that she was real, irrespective of what Russian space photography would have us believe. So fearful of another trip to the asylum for the criminally insane, he just did not tell anyone about her visits. Well, that's not really true. He did just mention it in passing to Brett and Nate who, being fearful of the same asylum, didn't mention it to anyone either.

Chuck had taught her to ride and had promised that the first foal to be born on his ranch would be kept especially for her. So she kept on going around and asking each horse in turn if it was pregnant. The horses, of course, did not answer her.

"I often wonder," said Chuck, "how the horses feel, to have a figment of my imagination riding around on their backs all day."

"Chuck," she said, "you know I'm real. I'm no different from anyone else that has a house on the Moon. Mind you, it is rather a big house."

"Daisy," he said, "I don't suppose figments mind being called Daisy, do they? I know I am insane, so don't try to make me believe I'm not." He paused for effect. "It's me trying to make me believe that I'm not nuts!"

"Hello Daisy," shouted Chuck's wife from the house, "have you got time for tea?"

"So," asked Daisy, "is Mavis nuts as well?"

"Always has been," smiled Chuck. "Always has been."

"Not today, Mrs Landers," shouted Daisy. "Another time if that's OK."

"Anytime," returned Mavis. "Why don't you bring your mother as well?"

Daisy liked Mavis, because the first time she had materialised accidently while Mavis was there, Mavis had just looked at her as if little girls appeared in front of her every day and said, "Well, I suppose this is Daisy, Chuck?" And when he had nodded, "Lemonade, Daisy?"

"Ooh, yes please," Daisy had said, and they had been firm friends ever since.

Before you ask how she knew about Daisy, you have to understand that Mavis is Chuck's wife and he loved her more than life itself, so he had told her everything. So when we say that Chuck 'didn't tell anyone', it goes without saying that Mavis was not included in that statement.

Daisy had made a couple of visits to Brett and Nate, but she had never been able to stop them from running away. She didn't want to carry on upsetting them so she stopped going and confined herself to her very pleasant visits with Chuck and Mavis.

"I will ask Mum," said Daisy, "but I am not sure she will be able to cope with the 'spatial distortion', as it's called. It takes some getting used to." She had resisted the temptation to say, 'spatial distortion as *Vana* called it', because she had not told Chuck about them yet.

"For now though, I really have to be going home...bye," she said and vanished.

"Bit disconcerting that," commented Mavis. "Always makes a mess of my hair."

●◐●◐●

Daisy normally used her garden as the platform for her travels, because from there she could not be overlooked. But now, for some reason, she materialised outside of Mrs Trent's front gate. That is, of course, Mrs Gladys Trent who lived at number sixteen.

"Whoops," she said, quickly looking around, but fortunately it did not look as if she had been seen. Then from the corner of her eye, she noticed a large backside sticking out of a side window of Mrs Trent's house and a small and wiry individual trying as hard as he could to shove it through.

"Excuse me, sirs," said Daisy in a firm, but reasonable tone of voice. "I am not sure that you should be doing that."

"What, who's that?" came a muffled voice from the other end of the backside.

"It's nobody," said the small and wiry individual, "only a nosey little girl. Don't worry. I'll deal with her."

"We," he announced officiously, "are government window inspectors. It is none of your business. Why don't you go home and play with a doll or something?"

"I'm sorry but I can't do that," said Daisy, continuing with the firm and reasonable. "I don't play with dolls. Also, I will have to ask my mother about 'Government Window Inspectors', as I have never heard of them. I live at number twelve, so is it alright with you if I yell very loud for my mum?"

"No, no, don't do that, little girl," said wiry hurriedly. "Let's make this our little secret. You see, we are really operatives for MI6."

"Of course," replied Daisy, "as long as you realise that I am 'Super Girl' and you are in real trouble."

While we realise that Daisy was telling the absolute truth, our burglar/GWI/MI6 agents just thought she was being sarcastic. Our small wiry individual released the large fat backside, which promptly fell back out of the window, and strode towards the gate. Daisy never moved as he approached. He reached inside his jacket, took out an identity wallet and waved it at her.

"This," he said, "says that I am MI6, and I shall have you arrested for interference with our investigations."

"How do I know that?" replied Daisy. "You are waving it around too much for me to read. You'll be OK then, with headlines in the paper…MI6 arrests innocent nine-year-old…will you?" She continued, "The article would continue, with information about your illegal search activities, and that the aforesaid nine-year-old caught you red-handed."

"The lady that lives in that house," said wiry, "is a Russian spy. She came into the European Union via Finland, and we have been tracking her for some time."

"I thought the Russians were our friends now," said Daisy, who was beginning to enjoy herself. She could not help but admire the inventiveness that the two burglars were employing. Oh, she was quite certain that they were neither Government Window Inspectors, nor MI6 operatives, but just ordinary burglars, quite nice, but burglars nonetheless.

"They are," said fat backside, who had recovered from his undignified exit from the house, "but that doesn't mean they don't spy on us, and we on them anyway."

Daisy thought of little old Mrs Trent and somehow could not picture her creeping across the Russian/Finnish border in the dead of night, or even of her doing anything that might be in any way devious. So she decided that it was time to give them a hand.

"Perhaps, if you," she said, pointing at wiry, "went through the window, and you," she said, pointing at fat backside, "were to push, perhaps you would have more success. If you like, I can keep a lookout for you."

"Hey, that's a good idea," said fat backside, "and then he can pull me in."

So that is what they did, and as soon as they were inside the house, Daisy sealed the door to the room and just simply made them unable to see the window. She then transmitted her voice via a mobile phone frequency to the emergency operator and reported a burglary in progress. She did quite enjoy it when the police came and the two were dragged, cursing and shouting, from the house in handcuffs.

The following day at breakfast, George who was reading the morning paper, exclaimed, "Hey, who would have thought that!"

"What's that, dear?" asked Marjorie.

"Well, it says here that two MI6 agents were arrested breaking into a house. Number sixteen in this street, in fact, and that subsequent investigations had led to a Mrs Trent, of that address, being detained on espionage charges. She's a Russian national apparently and came over from Finland. It seems her real name is Trentovovich."

A very red-faced Daisy quietly excused herself and slipped out into the garden.

Chapter Thirteen
Once Bitten

Daisy was a couple of days older, and keeping a very low profile after her huge mistake with the MI6 agents. She was extra careful not to let anything slip that in any way associated her with the fiasco. Marjorie, on the other hand, had over nine years' experience of a certain Miss Daisy Weal, and had noticed her sudden change in behaviour. She decided that if it was serious, then Daisy would confide in her. Daisy didn't, so she felt that there was no need to pursue the matter.

So, later that day, Daisy was idly sitting on the front wall of the garden swinging her legs and feeling decidedly sorry for herself. What had she achieved? A Mission Commander who thought he was insane; two crew members who had developed an irrational fear of one little girl; an aunt who was in jail in Canada; a milkman who had a pathological fear of flat things; a postman who had seen the inside of the jails of three countries; and a totally screwed up MI6 investigation.

And, she thought bitterly, *I'm only nine*.

"Yes, but you did straighten out two delinquents and one litter lout."

"True," she said, "not much compensation though."

She looked up and gazed into the seriously soulful, large brown eyes of a Boxer dog who was sitting in front of her. If she had not been on the wall, the dog, even sitting down, would have been larger than her. But he did look friendly and was sitting quite patiently.

"Well, hello there," she said. "What's your name?"

"Not very original, I'm afraid, it's Bruce. And you are Daisy Weal."

"Oh, come on, be reasonable," said Daisy. "I've seen that film on television, and it's fiction. Dogs can't talk."

"True, I mean, for instance, have you seen my mouth move?"

Just then, George must have seen the dog from the house, because he came hurtling down the front path brandishing a long-handled broom. He came out of the gate and with sweeping motions was trying to push a very confused Bruce away.

"Get away," he was shouting. "Scat, move."

"Dad," asked Daisy, "what exactly are you doing to my friend?"

"I would like to know that as well," thought Bruce.

George stopped. "Your friend?" he queried.

"Yes Dad, this is Bruce, and you really will upset him if you carry on waving that broom about."

George looked more closely at a very mournful Bruce and reconsidered his first impression of a mad wild dog savaging his only beloved daughter.

"Well, he did look a bit big from the house," he said in defence of his broom waving.

"That's because he is big," said Daisy. "We were starting to get to know one another, before this mad man charged him with a broom."

"Right then, sorry." He turned to Bruce. "Sorry Bruce."

"*No problem,*" thought Bruce, though only Daisy heard it, "*easy mistake to make.*"

George shouldered his broom and wandered back into the house.

●○◉○●

"Very odd," said Daisy. "Here I am, nine years old, and this is the first time that a dog has thought at me."

"*That's sixty-three in dog years,*" thought a very helpful Bruce. "*You just weren't listening,*" he continued. "*You're a person and you have been brought up to believe that dogs are, well, just dogs, so why would you be listening?*"

"OK," said Daisy. "So what's changed?"

"*The **Somethings** told us about you. You were sat on the wall feeling very sorry for yourself, and your mind was open.*"

"You know about the **Somethings**?" she asked in surprise.

"Yes, we do, it's only people that don't. Quite friendly things they are, you know. They try not to get us into trouble, but we do get blamed for their pranks sometimes. I don't blame them. They can't help it." He paused, and then said, *"I was looking for a bit of help really."*

"Well, you are quite big," said Daisy, "and you've got big teeth too, so how could little ol' me help you?"

"Well, it's my master. I really love him." There was a great sadness in his thoughts. *"I would die to protect him. I would really like to go everywhere with him, and be with him all the time. He pushes me away though, and makes me stay outside. Hits me sometimes and forgets my food quite often and doesn't change my water for days."*

She dropped down from the wall, walked up to Bruce and put her arms around his neck. She had to stretch up a bit, but Bruce helped by lowering his head a little.

"Oh! He does, does he?" she whispered into his ear. All self-pity had vanished and here was a determined and positive Daisy. She had heard the saying: 'Once bitten, twice shy' but on this day, and for this Daisy, it didn't apply. So what if she screwed up again; as long as it helped Bruce, who cared?

"Be careful," said Bruce. *"I can't help but protect him."*

"Don't worry," said Daisy. "He won't be hurt…well, not physically anyway."

"First though, you'll have to tell me where you live, and the villain's name. I don't like people who are nasty to dogs, and I like you. So this needs to be fixed, and fixed soon."

"Don't know numbers and such," thought Bruce, *"but I can show you. Everyone calls my master Andrew, Andrew Martin."*

Having been led to the house, which turned out to be number twenty-five and on the other side of the street, Daisy stood gazing at it. She let her mind wander into the house and saw the villain standing, talking into a telephone. He was only about five and a half feet tall with tight curly hair, and he seemed to be very annoyed with whoever he was talking to.

"Look," he was saying, "I know the money will be there. That's why I picked Friday. Just do your bit and everything will be fine. Make sure the car is a good one and don't forget the ski masks. I'll bring the guns."

Daisy quickly withdrew and turned to Bruce. "I'm sorry, Bruce, but he is far worse than we thought. I'm not sure he's going to be around to be your master for very long. He really is a criminal. I know you love him, but you are going to have to let him go. He isn't any good. And I'm not sure that there is anything I can do to make him any better."

An idea suddenly came to her. "Look, why don't you come and live with me?"

"I'd like that, but he would have to let me go. If he does, I'll miss him, but I can't stay with a bad person."

"Living with me will be nice. We'll hide all of the brooms from Dad, and I'm sure I can help you forget," said Daisy. "So, here goes nothing." And pushing open the gate, she strode up to the front door and rang the bell.

The door was wrenched open from the inside and an angry voice said, "WHAT?"

"Excuse me, sir," said Daisy. "I've been trying to find out who owns this big dog. He seems friendly enough—"

She was interrupted by Mr Martin, who shouted at Bruce and aimed a kick at him.

"There you are, you stupid mutt. Get around the back and stay there."

"He doesn't like to be kicked, and it's not nice. You don't deserve him," snapped Daisy.

"Who made you the RSPCA? He's a pain in the butt, and I'm fed up with him. You want him, you can have him." He reached inside the door, grabbed Bruce's lead and flung it at Daisy. "Now get out of here, both of you," he snapped and slammed the door.

Daisy picked up the lead and turned to Bruce. "Will that do, Bruce?" she asked.

"Yes, it will. Bit of a relief really."

"Hang on a minute though; there is something that I have to do." She reached for Mr Andrew Martin's mind and gently listened in on the thought that was planning the bank robbery. In the blink of an eye, she had it all. The time, the place, who his accomplice was and how much they hoped to gain.

"Come on, Bruce, let's go home." She turned and walked out of the gate with Bruce trotting happily at her side.

As they were walking, she contacted the emergency operator once again. She said that she didn't know whether it was true, but she had overheard these men talking about a bank robbery. She gave the operator all of the details as she had 'heard' them, and then broke the connection before awkward questions could be asked. They may think it odd that they could not trace the call, but…well, you can't have everything, can you? She knew that they would still follow up on the call because it held too much detail to be ignored.

She suddenly swivelled her head and looked across the road. She was convinced that she had just glimpsed someone, a small and wiry someone, disappearing around the corner. First checking for traffic, she ran over to look, closely followed by Bruce, but there was no one there.

"It's nothing, Bruce," she said, "I'm just going nuts."

They crossed back over the road and continued on their way home.

"Hey Mum," she shouted as they reached her house. "This is Bruce and he's coming to live with us."

Marjorie raised an eyebrow, turned and filled a bowl with water from the tap in the kitchen and put it down on the floor for Bruce.

"Hello Bruce," she said.

●●●●●

On the day of the bank robbery, two masked gunmen rushed into the bank, shouting, "This is a holdup. Everyone, get on the floor."

They were more than a little surprised when everyone did, with the exception of the six grim-looking officers of the Armed Response Unit. Andrew and his accomplice carefully put their weapons down on the floor and raised their hands.

To Daisy's way of thinking, jail was not sufficient punishment for such a nasty piece of work, so when the officer came to do his periodic check-up, the escape was discovered. The alarm was raised, but so far the notorious bank robber, Andrew Martin, has not been found. Oddly enough though, they did find a terrified little Spaniel cowering under the bed in the cell. But no one made any connection with the fact that on its collar there was a tag, and on the tag it said, 'Andrew'.

Chapter Fourteen
Of Witches and Warlocks

Daisy was almost nine and a half, not quite but almost, and over the past few days in the history lessons at school, she had been learning about the Inquisition. As can be imagined, for a young lady with the powers that Daisy had, this was a worry and caused quite a few sleepless nights.

"Mum, am I a witch?" she asked one morning.

"Good heavens, Daisy. Whyever should you think that?" exclaimed Marjorie.

"Well, I've got these powers, and that's what witches have, don't they?"

"You are my daughter, Daisy, and I would never give birth to a witch."

"Mum, be serious."

Marjorie sat down at the kitchen table and gazed at Daisy for what seemed like a long time.

"Witches," she said, "use potions, chant spells and wave magic wands around. You don't do any of those things. So no, I don't think you are a witch. I just think that you are my little girl, who happens to be gifted with amazing powers."

"Thanks, Mum, that helps," Daisy sighed.

"We do have a couple of witches living at number thirty-two, you know," said Marjorie.

"You know this for a fact!" exclaimed Daisy. "Why haven't they been burnt at the stake then?"

"Two reasons really, dear; firstly, we don't burn witches anymore, and secondly, they only play at it. They're not real witches."

"They have a son," she continued. "Odd little boy. He doesn't seem to play with other children. I don't think he's all there. Insists that he goes to school at some place called Hogwarts*, when in actual fact, he's at St Damien's Primary school."

*School for witches invented by J.K. Rowling.

"I've read about Hogwarts in a book. It's supposed to be a school for witches. Can't be that odd, if he reads the same books that I do," said Daisy. "Why haven't I seen him around?"

"Well, dear, you mostly play at the other end of the estate with Alfie, Jimmie and those nice Swain boys, so I don't suppose you've noticed him."

Daisy could see out of the kitchen window from where she was sitting, and she suddenly sat up straight. She had not been concentrating, but across the street she was convinced that briefly, she had seen someone half hidden behind a pillar box, someone who was small and wiry. She looked more closely, but whoever it had been, they were gone. *I'm starting to see things. This is the second time*, she thought, *it must be my conscience nagging me.*

"Are you alright, Daisy?" asked her mother.

"Yes, Mum, I'm fine. Is it OK if I go see Alfie?"

Marjorie did notice that Daisy and Bruce turned right out of the gate instead of left, but as she knew there was nothing on this Earth that could harm Daisy, she was not worried. *Gone witch hunting, I'll be bound*, she thought.

Mark and Angela Frogget, who lived at number thirty-two, were absolutely convinced that they were witches. The fact that none of their spells or potions ever worked, they put down to inexperience and lack of practice. So they practiced and practiced, and every day grew weirder and weirder.

Daisy and Bruce arrived at their gate as Angela Frogget rushed out of the house waving a stick at her son, Michael, who was in the garden. "*Levitalis*," she was screaming at him. She had heard the word or something similar somewhere, wanted to give it a try and wasn't too bothered that it sounded more like a medical remedy than a spell.

Daisy deduced her intentions from her thoughts and promptly raised Michael four feet above the ground. Angela fainted. Michael screamed and Daisy dropped him. *Whoops*, she thought, *this is fun*.

"*Is she alright?*" asked Bruce.

"I'd better go and check," said Daisy. "You sit out here and wait."

Bruce obediently sat just outside of the gate, in a position where Daisy would always be in his sight. "*I'll be watching*."

Daisy ran in through the gate and up to Angela, who was still lying unconscious on the ground. She knelt down and started to shake her.

"Wake up, wake up. Are you alright?"

Angela groaned, and then suddenly sat up straight. "It worked, it worked. For the first time, it's worked. It's true; we *are* witches."

She didn't seem to mind one little bit that Michael was howling and holding his backside, which actually was quite ample and couldn't possibly hurt as much as he would have her believe. Still, she was his mother, and who better to understand the desires for sympathy of an only child.

"Shut up, Michael," she said sympathetically. "Think yourself lucky it wasn't your head."

She was, of course, wrongly assuming that Michael had fallen because she had fainted and broken the spell.

"Who are you?" she asked, turning her attention to Daisy.

"I'm Daisy Weal from number twelve," said Daisy. "I saw you fall down and came in to help. I was out with my dog, Bruce," she continued by way of explanation and pointed towards the gate. "That's him, waiting for me."

"Looks big, I think he'll do fine just where he is," said Angela.

"Oh, but he's ever so friendly," insisted Daisy.

"Nevertheless...I don't do dogs. I am a cat person. Anyway, thank you very much for trying to help, little girl, but everything is under control now."

"Daisy," said Daisy, "I said my name was Daisy."

"Whatever," dismissed Angela. "You'd better go; your mother will be starting to worry."

I believe, thought Daisy, *that this place deserves several more visits.*

She collected Bruce and headed for home.

"What are you thinking, Bruce?" she asked, noticing that his face was just a bit more creased than normal.

"*I'm getting a bit worried*," he thought. "*I think I may be shrinking.*"

Daisy looked at him and laughed. "No, silly," she said, "I think I have entered a growth spurt as they call it. I'm getting bigger, you're not getting smaller."

"*Well, that's a relief,*" he said, shaking himself from head to toe.

She thought that it was really weird, how dogs' minds worked sometimes.

●◐◉◑●

Evenings were still light for quite a while at this time of year, so Daisy decided that after tea, she would go and give the Froggets a little more help in their efforts to become witches. She sneaked up to the front wall of the Froggets' house. It crossed her mind that with all this sneaking about that she had been doing lately, she was getting quite good at it, though it might get just a little harder now that she had a horse-sized companion.

"*Speak for yourself.*"

"Sorry, Bruce. Come on, let's settle down here by the wall, I have some concentrating to do."

She settled herself comfortably on the pavement with her back to the wall and closed her eyes. She didn't actually have to close her eyes, but a much more relaxed state of mind could be achieved by doing so.

"*Luminarthritis*," yelled Angela, waving her stick at the light switch.

Daisy obligingly turned on the lights.

"See Mark, I told you. I *am* a Witch…let me do something else."

"*Enteritis*," she said, pointing her 'wand' at the cupboard. The door opened and the plates sallied forth on their own into perfect places on the table.

"*Digitalism*!" And the television burst into life.

"Mum—" started Michael.

"*Silensium*," she shouted, and he suddenly found that he couldn't speak.

Daisy had to suppress a giggle at the made-up words that Angela was shouting. If there was such a thing as magic, they were probably the wrong words anyway.

Michael, being silent, had started to panic and wave his arms around, hoping to attract attention.

Mark, having had enough of his gesticulations, grabbed the 'wand' from Angela and shouted, "*Dormatorius*!" And Michael disappeared.

This is really good, he thought, but then as another possibility came to mind, he added, *I hope I actually did send him to his bedroom though and not somewhere else.*

"See," shrieked Angela in delight, "you are a Witch too."

"More accurately, a Warlock, love," replied Mark, who liked things to be precise.

"We can make money at this," declared Angela. "We can start witchcraft lessons."

So, wasting no time, they formed the Mark and Angela Frogget School of Witchcraft. You may think that people could not possibly be that gullible, but there was no shortage of pupils even at the *really* high fees that the Froggets charged. People flocked from all over the country to enrol, but unfortunately for Mark and Angela, their visions of fame and fortune never materialised. Very soon, the pupils started to become aware that they were not learning anything and all of the earnest demonstrations by their tutors never seemed to work, so a complaint was made to Trading Standards.

Apparently, according to Trading Standards, if you are a real witch and can prove it by making the inspector disappear or by performing some other miracle, it was OK in the eyes of the law. But you are not allowed to con people into believing that you are something that you definitely are not. Therefore, because they insisted that they were witches but couldn't prove it, they were arrested on charges of misleading the public.

The court case was brief, they were found guilty and as the judge described them as barking mad in his summing up, they were remanded to a psychiatric unit for 'an unspecified term'. Michael was sent, much to his delight it has to be said, to a Foster home.

Daisy was satisfied. They were being punished. She hadn't decided yet how long she would let it go on for, but for now they were being punished. She felt that it was well-deserved because she was not happy, not happy at all, with people who didn't do dogs.

Chapter Fifteen
A Record for George

The Froggets had been sent to a psychiatric unit for an indefinite period, but the morning after they had been locked up, they were still being visited by the police. The thrust of the questioning was directed at the mysterious disappearance of all the money that had been collected in advance bookings. The Froggets, who had a slightly bent remote cousin, pretended total ignorance and the questioning was eventually abandoned.

The same morning, Daisy was still in bed, and fully intending to stay there for as long as possible. It was Saturday after all and there was no school, so she could be forgiven a little laziness. Marjorie, however, was sitting in the kitchen and was very puzzled.

She had been watching the weather forecast on the little flat screen television that folded down from the underside of the cabinets. Rain had been forecast for everywhere, but not, it seemed, in Daisy Weal County where sunshine was expected for the foreseeable future. This had brought home to Marjorie the fact that it had actually not rained here in months.

"Daisy," she shouted, "get down here at once. You have some explaining to do."

A bleary-eyed Daisy, still in pyjamas that had a panda motif on the front, appeared at the door followed closely by an equally bleary-eyed Bruce. Bruce, it has to be said, could have slept wherever he liked but he had chosen never to leave Daisy's side and slept in her room, always watching, always protecting. If she had been given time to wake up properly, she might have been forewarned. She might even have picked up the thoughts of her impending doom.

"Morning, Mum."

"Sit," Marjorie commanded, and Bruce decided that he needed to go outside.

Now Daisy was wide awake. She probed briefly and realised that she had been found out, so she opened up those big green eyes, put on her most innocent look and turned her gaze towards her mother. Mother, however, was not fooled.

"Daisy," she said, "would you know anything about all the rain we are not having?"

"Er...no," she started, and then really noticed her mother's look. "Well...yes."

"Explain now, and live for another day," commanded Marjorie.

"Well, I actually like the sunshine, and I really hate to be wet. It's supposed to be summer and Bruce and I like to go out without getting soggy."

"Daisy, don't you realise how irresponsible that is! Farmers need the rain for their crops. Gardeners need the rain. Reservoirs need rain to keep topped up. Rain cleans things, freshens things. You can't stop rain because things die, like plants and wild animals. The great joy is its unpredictability and you really cannot interfere with that." She relented a little. "And besides which, without weather, what would we English have to talk about?"

"OK Mum, I'm sorry. I never thought, and I suppose it was selfish of me," said Daisy, and suddenly, not very far away, came a clap of thunder.

Within minutes, the heavens opened, and down it came. The accompanying thunderstorm was a site to behold. Flash after flash, and an almost continuous rumble of thunder, punctuated by the resounding 'crack' of a really close one. About an hour later, it moved on, leaving the freshness in the air that can only be found after a really good thunderstorm. The road was still awash with water, but that would drain away soon enough. There were only a few people fortunately who hadn't managed to make shelter and were soaked, as Marjorie would say, right through to their knickers. The sun came out again, but everywhere stayed too wet for Daisy's liking, so she found a pile of DVDs and settled down for a day of relaxation and entertainment. Bruce happily lay down beside her.

● ● ● ● ●

The next day was warm, sunny and certainly a lot dryer, but as Daisy and Bruce were about to go out, Daisy was informed that: "Your father is playing golf today. You can go and take Bruce if you like, but make sure he understands that he cannot eat the golf balls. And he mustn't fetch any."

"I don't remember Dad ever playing golf," commented Daisy. "I've seen it on telly, and it looks ever so hard. Are you sure he knows how? And why do *we* have to go?"

"Because I'm your mother and I say so, that's why," declared Marjorie.

"Err...OK Mum," said Daisy, who was old enough, and wise enough, to understand a command when she heard one. "Do you want to go and watch Dad play golf, Bruce?" she asked.

"*Will it be OK if I chase rabbits?*"

"As long as they aren't carrying golf balls," she replied.

"You keep talking to that dog," said Marjorie, "does he know what you are talking about?"

"Of course, he does. We have quite long and interesting conversations, but sometimes he's a bit weird though."

"*Speak for yourself,*" grumbled Bruce.

"I don't doubt that for a minute," said Marjorie.

So when George came downstairs with his golf bag slung over his shoulder, Daisy and Bruce were ready and waiting by the car.

"Oh, I'm taking an audience, am I?" he asked.

"Yes Dad, but don't worry, I am absolutely sure that you are brilliant at golf."

"Golfer...brilliant golfer," he corrected. "Better than I am at darts, you can be sure of that. You'll have to make allowances though, because I haven't played for ages."

Marjorie had told Daisy that George was playing one of the senior managers from work, so Daisy thought it best to ask: "What do the politics say, Dad? Is it OK to win, or do you have to lose to keep your job?"

"Don't like the man," stated George emphatically, "but fortunately, he's not my line Manager. His name is Cyril Foster." He grinned. "Make sure you are polite to him, while I am doing my very best to humiliate him."

"Oh," said Daisy, "I'm sure you will, Dad, I'm sure you will."

They finally arrived at St Damien's Golf course, which was just past the Primary school at the end of St Damian's Rise. It had been looking a bit brown after so long without rain, but after yesterday, it was certainly perking up a bit.

George took Daisy to the Clubhouse and introduced her to Cyril, who they found propping up the bar. A scruffy individual, he was tall and lanky with untidy hair, who did not attempt to hide his distaste as he spotted Daisy.

"Well, are you ready, Weal? Let's get started," said Cyril, completely ignoring her.

Hole one was 398 yards from the tee to the hole, and the normal number of shots required to reach it was set at four, which in golf speak, made it a par four. Daisy firmly believed that Albatrosses, Eagles and Birdies all had wings and flew about in the sky. So the fact that they were also all golfing terms left her a just a little confused and convinced her that people who played golf were pretty strange.

Cyril thought he did very well to complete the hole in six shots, and was less than delighted when George hit a one under par three. As the game progressed and George miraculously managed a one under par for each hole, Cyril became more and more agitated. Consequently, his game, which was not particularly good at the best of times, got worse, with the last par four ending up for him as a nine. He was seriously peeved at the tenth hole when George's final putt, while at least two feet wide of the hole, suddenly turned sharp left and dropped in.

"How did you do that, Weal?" he spluttered. "It's not possible."

"I think it's all in the ball's spin and the lie of the ground. Wind helps a bit too," waffled George, who had absolutely no idea how it had happened either.

Bruce had decided not to chase rabbits today because this was much too interesting, so he happily wandered along behind everyone else.

By the time they reached the fourteenth hole, Cyril was glowering and not talking at all, and so it continued for the next three holes.

Then they arrived at the final tee and George managed, with the help of Daisy, a hole in one on the last par three, completing the round in nineteen under par, which was a course record by twelve shots. On the basis of George's performance, all of the holes for this particular golf course were later reassessed and their par values in some cases reduced.

As they approached the clubhouse, Daisy suddenly noticed a face watching from a window. It was a face she recognised as belonging to a small and wiry individual, but when she looked again, the face was gone. She quickly searched for thoughts, any thoughts, but there were none, so she smoothed the puzzlement from her face and followed her father into the clubhouse.

George's fame had preceded him and he was welcomed into the clubhouse as a hero but Cyril, on the other hand, was totally ignored. Some of George's joy trickled away when he was politely informed that he had performed brilliantly, particularly his hole in one at the last. He would, they said, be delighted to know that by tradition, it required that he buy drinks for everyone.

No one ever found out how everyone in the company eventually received the same email, which gave a blow-by-blow description of George's triumph. Daisy, however, just smiled quietly to herself. To George's absolute delight, Cyril Foster was so humiliated that he could not handle it and resigned from the board, leaving the company shortly afterwards. This left a vacancy and as George was the hero of the moment, what better person was there to offer it to.

The promotion and raise in salary came just in time to repair the hole that tradition had made in his credit card. As a bonus, it also bought a new outfit for Marjorie, a laptop for Daisy and a new collar and lead for Bruce. George didn't need to buy anything for himself, as he was still basking in the glory that Daisy had provided for him. You could say that George was satisfied, very satisfied indeed.

Chapter Sixteen
Revelation

Bruce nudged Daisy with his nose. "*Time to get up,*" he thought.

"Yuk," said Daisy out loud, "do you really have to nudge me with that soggy nose? Can't you use a nice dry paw, or something else?"

"*Nope,*" thought Bruce, "*it's what we dogs do. No control over the paws, you see. Might accidentally scratch you.*" He continued, "*And one of our little pleasures in life is sticking a soggy nose into a human's ear.*" He paused, considering, "*I suppose I could lick you instead.*"

"Do that in the morning," declared Daisy, "and you become a hotdog."

"*What's a hotdog?*" asked Bruce. "*Is it something that I'd like?*"

"It's a sausage in a bread roll," explained Daisy.

"*Oh-er,*" thought Bruce, "*is it OK if I nudge you somewhere else instead then?*"

"Yes," said Daisy, "as long as it's not ear, eye, nose or mouth."

By this time, Daisy had washed her face at the little wash basin next to the bed and then cleaned her teeth. Wriggling out of her pyjamas, she reached for her favourite T-shirt (the one with a large Bruce lookalike on the front).

"Why am I doing this?" she asked Bruce. "There's a much quicker way."

Letting herself relax, she reached into the right place in her mind and was instantly dressed in her favourite jeans, T shirt and red and white sneakers.

"Technical problem her though," she told Bruce, and then sat down to put her sneakers on the right feet, "I do believe more practice may be required."

Satisfied that everything was now on correctly, she led Bruce down to the kitchen, where they found George in a very cheerful mood.

"Start packing," he said, "we are off on holiday. I can afford it now with the extra money I get from the promotion, and besides which, I am due a couple of weeks off, so I've booked them to start next Monday. It's Tuesday today, so we don't have much time to book it or even decide where we want to go. Anyone got any preferences?"

"I don't mind," said Marjorie, "anywhere will do, as long as I don't have to cook and clean."

She turned towards Daisy. "Anywhere special for you, dear?"

Daisy started to open her mouth, and then closed it. She had been tormented for a long time by the fact that she knew her father had always thought she was special, but she also knew that he had never known just how very special she really was. She looked towards Marjorie with a question in her eyes, and the slightest of nods from her mother was enough.

"I would like to spend a couple of weeks at Chuck Landers' ranch," said Daisy, and then continued, "Mavis did invite you both."

"Who he, and who her?" asked George, then his eyes opened as the penny dropped. "Wait a minute. He's that astronaut who they thought had gone round the bend, isn't he? Come on, Daisy," he chided, "be sensible now. How do we know he's got a ranch, and how can we contact him in time? And anyway, why would he want a trio of mad English people visiting him?"

"He's my friend," said Daisy, "and I could go and a—"

"Daisy, that's enough." interrupted George. "Let's live in the real wo—"

He was stopped by Marjorie who said, "George, *listen* to her."

George looked up into Marjorie's eyes and saw how serious she was. He could also see that there was intensity to her words that he had not seen before, and the strain in her face was clearly visible.

"What's the matter, love?" he asked softly.

"Listen to your daughter, George, *really* listen, and don't interrupt."

George turned to Daisy. "Is there something here that I don't know about?" he asked.

"Yes Daddy," said a very meek Daisy. "I *can* go and ask Chuck wherever he is in the world, and it will only take a second."

"I think you're pulling my leg, not sure yet why, but I'll play along," said George patiently. "OK then, go ahead." And Daisy vanished.

Marjorie had never heard George swear in all of the years that she had known him, so she was very surprised when, staring at the place where Daisy had stood, he muttered something very rude. He then looked at Marjorie and she saw light dawning in his eyes.

"The liquorice tree?" he asked.

"Yes," she said, "and the Milkman; the Postman; the Swain boys; the green-face epidemic; the wannabe witches; and the MI6 agents, just to name a few."

"@#*!*#@," muttered George again, "and she was involved in that Lunar disaster and that's how she knows Chuck Landers, I suppose?"

"I do believe so. She was the one who saved their lives," said Marjorie. "Since then, she visits him quite often at his ranch in America, and talks a lot about his wife, Mavis. What you really, really don't know," she continued, "is that she and Bruce think at each other. Well, Bruce thinks, but Daisy prefers to talk out loud."

"Really, really," he muttered, "I obviously don't know anything."

There was a pop and Daisy reappeared in front of him. "Chuck said next Monday would be fine. He can easily accommodate us, he says, and he would love to meet someone who could give birth to a figment of his imagination." Then she added, "Mavis told him not to be silly, and that she can't wait until Monday."

"We have a few things to talk about, Daisy," said George, "but at the moment, I probably wouldn't be able to cope with the answers. I reckon that I'm probably nuts or dreaming... I presume we'll be flying 'Air Daisy' or something on Monday."

"I can move really big objects," said Daisy, "but moving people over long distances is slightly different, so to be on the safe side, I'll move you both one at a time." Then she added, "I told Chuck about Bruce, and he is happy for him to come as well."

The following few days were a bit of a whirlwind as clothes were packed and the house was cleaned. When Monday arrived, Marjorie insisted that before they went, clean beds were made available for their return. Daisy enthusiastically lined up the cases after all of the chores were finished, and then George, Bruce and finally, Marjorie. She explained that the cases were easy to move, but George would need to be there first so that he could look after Bruce while she returned for Marjorie.

"Do I need my passport?" he asked.

"Shut up, George," said Marjorie, withering him with a look.

He looked suitably chastened and then winced when there was a loud pop as Daisy and the luggage vanished.

"Perhaps I'll get used to this in time," he muttered.

"I doubt it, George, I really do doubt it."

And he jumped again as, with a pop, Daisy reappeared. "OK Dad, it's your turn. Hold your breath and close your eyes, 'cos the spatial distortion isn't nice. It will be pretty quick though."

"Oh God!" said George, taking a deep breath and closing his eyes. He felt a peculiar twisting pins and needles sensation and a sudden jerk.

"OK Dad, you're here. You can open your eyes now."

George warily opened his eyes to find himself standing in front of a quite strikingly beautiful young lady and a tall man who appeared to be in his middle to late thirties.

"This is my dad, George," she said, "and Dad, this is Chuck and Mavis."

"Pleased to meet you, Chuck," said George, holding out his hand.

Chuck took the hand and then pumped it up and down with some enthusiasm. "At last, we meet," he said. "Great to see you, George."

But then both he and George jumped as Daisy disappeared with a pop.

"I can't believe that I'm surrounded by wimps," observed Mavis.

No more than five seconds later, a second pop brought Daisy and Bruce into view, with Bruce promptly falling on his nose as he appeared. The sudden appearance, even though they were expecting it, caused an already nervous George and Chuck to jump again like a pair of startled rabbits.

"*That doesn't do much for a dog's legs, or his dignity,*" Bruce thought at Daisy. "*Remind me to be lying down next time.*"

"So this is the famous Bruce," said Mavis, bending down to him.

"Woof!" barked Bruce, and then proceeded to provide her with a maxi lick all over her face.

"I think we'll get on just fine, Bruce, unless you drown me first," she said, lifting her head out of his range. "I'll get you some water after Marjorie arrives."

"Back in a tick," said Daisy.

George and Chuck braced themselves and as she popped out of existence, Chuck grabbed George's arm and said, "Fancy a tour around the ranch, George…like now…quick."

"Absolutely," replied George as Chuck literally dragged him away for the impromptu tour, "anywhere as long as we aren't here when she comes back. I will never get used to that."

A couple of minutes later, Daisy reappeared with a completely unflappable Marjorie standing serenely beside her.

"Marjorie!" yelled Mavis, launching herself and throwing both arms around Marjorie. "Daisy has told me so much about you, and I have been dying to meet you. Come to the house, we've so much to talk about and I'd love to show you around." She paused to take a breath and then said apologetically, "I'm sorry, but I think I'm babbling."

"Don't worry," replied Marjorie, "as long as it's OK for me to babble as well, and it is nice to meet you after hearing so much from Daisy." She paused and looked around. "Where have the men disappeared to?"

"Supposedly on a tour, but really hiding from Daisy; can't take the popping in and out, pair of wimps if you ask me."

"I will say in George's defence that he only found out on Tuesday. But yes, I think wimp is an apt description."

Mavis linked her arm through Marjorie's and then said, "Come on, Bruce, let's get that water for you."

He woofed in appreciation and she marched them all towards the house. Daisy hung back a little, wondering what sort of can of worms she had opened in introducing Mavis to her mother. *Will I be able to cope with them both together*, she asked herself as she watched them arm in arm, bouncing towards the house, seeming to be more like sisters than people who had only just met. *Oh well, I did it to myself*, she thought, and quickened her pace to catch them up.

"Come along, Daisy, no dawdling," commanded Mavis.

The next two weeks passed faster than any of them really wanted. Mavis and Marjorie had gossiped for endless hours, and George and Chuck had spent equally endless hours around the ranch and off to the nearby creek to fish. Daisy attempted to divide her time between both of her parents, but as they were so far apart for most of the time, she completely failed and ended up virtually living with the horses. What made matters worse was being totally ignored by Bruce who, she suspected, had fallen hopelessly in love with Mavis, mainly because he just lay there looking at her for hours on end.

But all good things must come to an end and thus so did the holiday. Daisy transported their luggage home and then waited patiently while all the emotional farewells were said, and the four new friends finally managed to drag themselves apart. Bruce just made moon eyes at Mavis and kept going back to lick her again.

"You must come and see us in England," said George, "we'll book you with 'Daisy Air'."

"Love to!" chorused Chuck and Mavis.

"Bye," said Daisy, beginning to lose patience. But she was about to launch herself and George when she saw *him* standing by the stables. There was no mistaking the small and wiry man standing there looking at her. Daisy reacted immediately and was at the stables virtually before she thought about going. She quickly looked around, but whoever it had been, they were now gone. She ran into each stall in turn, but apart from horses, they were all empty. *I will find him eventually*, she thought. *I know I'm not seeing things.*

She returned to the four who were so engrossed in their farewells that it was obvious that they hadn't missed her at all.

"Bye, we're off," she said again and then launched George and herself for home. Two more quick journeys and everyone was safely returned to twelve Trendal Place.

"Daisy," asked Marjorie, "who was that man I saw at the stables? You know, the one you flashed off to see."

Daisy sighed. She should have known that her mother would have noticed.

"He was gone when I got there," she explained. "He keeps popping up, but I don't know who he is…yet."

She hadn't thought that her mother had been watching, but her mind went back a few years to when she had been told, after a particularly sneaky episode, that mothers can see through walls and around corners.

Scary, she thought, *that really is scary.*

Chapter Seventeen
'Bin' to New York

Daisy was a couple of weeks older when the United States of America became the focus of a geography lesson. More specifically, it was New York that was the subject of this particular lesson, and the teacher, who was of American extract, began with some enthusiasm. Firstly, she described how the city was built around a central park, and then went on to explain that it was the largest city in the world that you could not get lost in. In response to eager questions on how this could be true, she continued with a detailed explanation of the city's layout, of numbered avenues and cross streets. Because it was a subject obviously dear to the teacher's heart, her enthusiasm rubbed off onto the children, especially Daisy, who vowed to visit the city at her first opportunity.

So the next few days were taken up by eager young minds in discussion on how great it would be to go there. No matter what class they were in or what the subject was, the teachers stood no chance. It was talk about New York or nothing got done. So each teacher told about the various places that they had been to and described what they had seen. Over a few days, a picture began to emerge of what the true New York was really like. All of this continual discussion only served to make Daisy more determined than ever to experience it for herself. So one Saturday morning at breakfast, she asked, "Mum, what would I have to take if I went to New York, and would I need a foreign language, like American, for instance?"

"Well, at this time of year, it is quite warm, so no special clothes," said Marjorie who, to her credit, felt questions were not required. "You won't need a foreign language because they speak English, though there are a few differences. Like sidewalk instead of pavement; elevator instead of lift; truck instead of lorry; gas instead of petrol. There are quite a lot, but I'm sure you'll peek into their minds to understand," she continued. "When were you thinking of going?"

"I thought today would be good," declared Daisy.

"Well, don't forget that they are five hours behind of us, or ahead of us…never could figure out which, so you'll have to take that into consideration… I think it's behind," Marjorie concluded.

"So if I left here at three in the afternoon, I would get there at ten in the morning?" asked Daisy.

"Probably," said Marjorie, "but you get back here by ten pm our time at the latest. Now promise me that you will. That's still pretty late, but it's not a school day tomorrow so you can sleep in. It'll still give you seven hours there."

"OK Mum, I'll go and rest in my room until three, but I'm sure I won't need seven hours there."

Marjorie did not voice any objections because she was well aware of the extent of Daisy's capabilities. In fact, she suspected that her daughter's powers might be much greater than even she realised, but being a mother, she knew she would still worry until Daisy returned.

"Remember that the traffic drives on the right, so be careful."

"Righto, Mum," said Daisy as she mounted the stairs to her room.

Daisy got more and more excited as three o'clock approached. Finally, she could wait no longer and slipped on her anorak, reached into her mind, oriented her destination and launched. She materialised in the middle of the pedestrian area of Times Square. One man on a skateboard ran into a set of traffic lights. Another, on roller blades, tripped on the kerb and demolished two tables laden with coffee, leaving the drinkers reaching for non-existent cups. Two cyclists collided, an elderly woman fainted and two people crossing against the lights narrowly escaped death from a chauffeur-driven limousine. Almost everyone else had also seen her appear and were obviously in various stages of shock.

Daisy instinctively did a reality shift and for a moment, it felt as if a thousand needles had passed through her. She avoided being violently sick by a whisker, as everything shimmered as if seen through a heat haze and then sharply snapped back into focus.

She hadn't done that before and although it was quite unpleasant, she was quite pleased with the results. *OK*, she thought, *avoid doing that too often.*

It was as if she had always been there. A man on a skateboard skilfully avoided a set of traffic lights and zoomed on up Broadway, while another on roller blades jumped the kerb, weaved through the tables, rocketed past Macy's and on up Seventh Avenue. Two cyclists waved as they passed each other on Forty-Second. An elderly woman, and two other people, waited for the lights to change before crossing the road, hardly noticing the chauffeur-driven limousine. No one else noticed anything at all.

Daisy turned slowly around and was suitably impressed by the giant video screens that adorned most of the buildings, so she sat down onto a nearby seat and admired them for a while. Though she was a little saddened by the story that was featured on one large screen. It was about three little girls who had been missing for six days and were still the subject of a nationwide manhunt. Then, conscious as she was that she had a lot to see in a fairly short time, she set off down Seventh Avenue and headed for Thirty-Fourth Street. She had learnt at school that the Empire State building was somewhere down that way between Fifth and Sixth Avenues and she badly wanted to see it.

She was beginning to believe by the time that she reached Thirty-Four that the New Yorkers took their life in their hands every time they crossed the road. She couldn't quite understand why cars that were turning into a street from an Avenue could do so whilst the pedestrian lights crossing the street showed the walking man. Being small, she narrowly missed being squashed quite a few times even though it was her right of way. She also had to dodge several times to avoid people pushing trolleys laden with food, or large bottles of water in plastic crates, and even one man pushing a hospital patient hoist. The oddest thing that she noticed was that there were virtually no children. In particular, she saw no young teenagers or babies in prams, except once when she glimpsed two women each pushing a buggy with seats facing outwards for six children.

Finally, she made it in one piece and turned down Thirty-Fourth Street towards Sixth Avenue, which she discovered was called the Avenue of the Americas. Then, towering above her, she saw the Empire State Building.

Wow, she thought, *now that is tall*.

For all practical purposes, Daisy could do anything she wanted and was sorely tempted to jump to the top, but then she spotted the sign that told her of the cost for children to visit the observation deck. Having no American money with her, she decided that suddenly appearing up there to avoid the charge might be dangerous; not for her but for anyone who might witness her appearance.

Maybe next time, she thought.

"Are you lost, little girl?" a rather unpleasant voice asked from behind her.

"No," said Daisy firmly and, spotting a woman coming towards her, continued, "That's my mum coming now."

As the woman came level with them, she turned and walked along beside her, and then kept with her as the woman turned up Sixth Avenue.

After they crossed over Fifty-Second street, the woman stopped and, turning towards Daisy, asked, "Are you OK, little girl?"

"Yes," said Daisy firmly, "I'm over from England and I was just out for a walk when a man spoke to me. He didn't seem nice, so I tagged on to you. Sorry."

"That's OK, my name's Candy-Anne. I'm just on my way to Starbucks for coffee. Want a soda? You can join me if you like."

"I would like that," said Daisy. "My name's Daisy."

"Pleased to meet you, Daisy," replied Candy-Anne. "Where are you staying?"

Daisy pointed at what looked like a hotel a little further up Sixth Avenue and said, "That one, my mum did tell me its name, but I can't remember."

"Oh!" said Candy-Anne. "That's the Hilton. It's near Fifty-Fourth, so let's go into that Starbucks on the corner of Fifty-Sixth."

Daisy spent a very pleasant half hour chattering to Candy-Anne while they were in Starbucks, and consumed more Diet Pepsi than was good for her. At least, that's what she knew her mother would say. She was really beginning to like Candy-Anne, so she asked where she lived and if she would like to keep in touch.

"I know I'm only a kid," said Daisy, "but my mum thinks I'm a sensible one, so I would really like to write to you if that's OK."

"You know, Daisy," said Candy-Anne, "I really would like that, and it's been fun talking with you. I'm a visitor here myself, you know, so I'll write my address down. My folks live in Hawaii. Well, my dad originally came from Kentucky, but he got smitten by this Hawaiian hula dancer. He stayed in Hawaii, she gave up hula dancing and they got married."

She took a small notebook from her purse, quickly wrote her name and address on the first page, tore it out with a blank sheet and passed them both together with the pen to Daisy. Daisy very carefully wrote her own details down on the blank sheet and passed it and the pen back to Candy-Anne.

"I've got to go now, Daisy. It's not far to the hotel, sure you'll be OK?"

"Oh sure!" said Daisy. "I'll be fine now, thank you. I'll write soon... Bye."

She watched as Candy-Anne hurried off down the avenue and was about to turn to walk in the opposite direction when a hand grabbed her arm.

"You're coming with me. Keep your mouth shut and don't try that mother trick on me again."

Daisy looked up into unpleasant voice's face and decided that it was probably more unpleasant than his voice. She probed his mind and recoiled with shock. He was disgusting. Full of evil thoughts of the very nasty things that he intended to do to her, and in fact had already done to other little girls. There were even visions of a locked room and the horrible secret that it held. In her nine years, Daisy had not even sensed such an evil mind, and up until now had not thought that such a mind could actually exist. She was repelled and afraid, but most of all angry, very, very angry.

"Wrong person," she said calmly. "This time, you've picked the wrong little girl. You are an evil man and you don't deserve to carry on walking around."

"Hah!" he laughed. "And what are you gonna do about it, eh?"

"I won't kill you," said Daisy, "but you might wish that I had."

He lifted his hand as if to strike her, but the blow never landed and he vanished, vanished into an outside place, where Daisy had said no one would want to be. Daisy stood trembling. She looked up and across the street, then started as she saw a small wiry man watching her. He looked straight at her, smiled and nodded his head in approval, before slowly fading and finally disappearing from view. That smile and the nod lifted away her fear of who, or what, he was. She now knew that he was no threat to her, so she quickly dismissed him and thought, *One more thing left to do*.

●●●●●

On the other side of New York, in an abandoned building, there was a locked room in the basement, and in it were three terrified little girls. The room was bare except for a dirty mattress on the floor on which the three huddled, trying desperately to comfort each other. They started to cry and gripped each other more tightly as suddenly they heard bolts being withdrawn on the door. One of them whimpered as the lock snapped as it was opened and the door swung inwards. There was no one there, but a soft voice, a little girl's voice, whispered, "Don't be afraid. He won't come back. You can go home now, just follow my voice and then find a policeman."

They followed the soft voice and strangely did not worry that they could not see anyone, just a feeling of intense relief at being free after so many days. Finally, they emerged into the open air, almost immediately saw a police car and waved it down. The police in the car managed to piece together from the rush of words from all three at once that they were the girls who had been previously reported missing and were the subject of a still ongoing national alert.

The abandoned building became the focus of attention, with police lying in wait for the villain and searching for the little girl with the English accent who had rescued the trio. They never did find her and the villain never returned, so eventually the surveillance was called off, but three sets of parents would never forget, and be forever grateful, that a little English girl had visited New York.

If you visit New York, you may notice a large new rubbish bin on the corner of Fifty-Sixth Street and Sixth Avenue, but what you will not know is that it is silently screaming and screaming, and quite, quite insane.

Chapter Eighteen
Where Is Coventry?

It was Sunday, and as Daisy slowly returned from a deep and satisfying sleep after the previous day's excitement in New York, she automatically glanced at the clock and sat bolt upright.

"Eleven-thirty," she yelled. "Bruce…"

Then she noticed that Bruce was not in his normal place on the bed, but was laying way across the room in the corner. He lay with his head on his paws, looking at her in a way that could only be described as disapproving.

"Why didn't you wake me up, Bruce?" she asked. "It's almost afternoon."

"*Hrmph*," thought Bruce and got up and stalked out of the room.

Daisy hopped out of her bed and rushed out into the bathroom. There was a number of loud clattering and swishing sounds, the sound of a toilet flushing and then Daisy flew, literally it must be said, back to her bedroom. Clothes went in all directions, the bed made itself and the room became clean and tidy as Daisy emerged from it fully dressed.

In the few seconds that she had taken to complete her morning tasks, Bruce had disappeared downstairs, not waiting for her as he usually did, and she heard her mother open and then close the front door.

"Don't stay out all day," she heard her say, "bark when you come back, and don't scratch the door."

Daisy hurried downstairs and into the kitchen.

"Where's Bruce gone, Mum? Why didn't he wait for me?" she asked. "He wouldn't speak to me this morning, or wait. What's up with him?"

"Did you say anything to him when you came back from New York?" asked Marjorie.

"Well, I ruffled his ears and said 'Hello Bruce'." She paused in reflection and continued, "I think he just 'har-rumphed', but I wasn't really paying attention."

"Ah!" said Marjorie. "I do suspect that you have been sent to Coventry."

"What?" protested Daisy. "But no one has sent me anywhere. I am still here. Why do I have to go there, and anyway, where is it?"

"Coventry is in the Midlands," explained Marjorie. "But it is just a saying. When no one talks to you, it's called being sent to Coventry. And before you ask, I have no idea why."

"But why won't Bruce talk to me? What have I done?"

"Well, let me see now," said Marjorie. "Perhaps it has something to do with the fact that his whole world revolves around you, and in return you…" She held up her fingers. "One…swanned off to New York without even letting him know what you had planned… Two…didn't even say good-bye… Three…and most important, didn't take him with you…and Four…ruffled his head and said 'Hello Bruce' when you returned." Scornfully, she continued, "Ruffled his head? What's that all about? Bruce would lay his life down for you, and you *ruffle* his head."

Daisy sat looking at her mother and tears began to trickle down her cheeks. Muffling a sob, she said, "I didn't realise, Mum. I didn't think. Will he forgive me?"

"I don't know, Daisy. Maybe if you find him, hug him, say sorry to him and promise never to do it again, you just might be lucky. That dog worships the ground you walk on. Perhaps you should give him the same consideration."

Fighting back her tears, Daisy got up. "Where's he gone, Mum? Is he in the garden?"

"No, Daisy, he's not. I let him out of the front door and he ran up the road."

"I'll find him, Mum, I've got to," she sobbed. "And I'll beg him to forgive me, and if he does, then I'll never go anywhere without him again."

Daisy ran out of the house and into the street. She brought all of her formidable power to bear and channelled it into listening to the thoughts and emotions that swirled about her. She 'heard' the complex sounds of human thoughts, the simpler ones of dogs and cats and the more instinctive levels of smaller mammals. It was an enormous inrush of thought that for a moment threatened to overwhelm her. But she quickly brought the volume down to a bearable level and began sifting through it, isolating and examining each thought before filtering it out of her mind. Bruce seemed to be nowhere.

Daisy realised that to open her mind to the entire world, or even to her whole county, would overload even her ability, so she extended her search outwards a small piece at a time.

Suddenly, there was a mind that she recognised and as she paused, it felt her touch and recoiled slightly before it, in turn, recognised her.

"*Hello Daisy, is that you?*" came a thought from Chuck Landers. "*You haven't done this before, is something wrong?*"

"*Bruce...he's gone... I upset him...and he ran away...and now I can't find him.*" Her thoughts faltered, reflecting her feelings of panic and distress.

"*It's OK, Daisy. You'll find him... But don't waste your time searching so far away.*"

"*But I've searched all of England...and he's gone.*"

"*How have you arranged your search?*"

"*All the thoughts of everything... I've listened until my head hurts...even to birds and things...he's just gone.*"

"*What if he's asleep, Daisy?*"

For a second there was silence, and then her thoughts roared into Chuck's head, literally thumping him onto his backside into a pile of horse manure that he had been clearing.

"*Of course, thank you, thank you, I love you, Chuck... When I'm big, you can divorce Mavis and marry me.*"

"*Whoa girl, you could explode a person that way...as they say '**softly, softly, catchee monkey**'.*"

"*Who does? Why? Oh, never mind, sorry for the shout, I'll let you know when I find him. Bye.*"

It was with some relief that Chuck realised he was once again alone with his horse manure.

Daisy sat down on the wall by her gate and recommenced her search, but this time she was looking for quieter thoughts, softer thoughts, unconscious thoughts and especially dreams.

Then she felt it, softly at first, a tiny thought from a mind that she knew, and as she focussed on it, it grew stronger and stronger and she touched it, and it was Bruce. As Chuck had guessed, he was asleep and Daisy quickly withdrew so as not to wake him. She leapt to her feet and raced down the road. She knew where he was. He was asleep under a tree in the woods by St Damien's golf course. As soon as she was clear of the houses and not easily visible, she launched in mid-stride and in the blink of an eye, was in the woods racing towards the still sleeping Bruce.

She flung herself at him, throwing her arms around him and sobbing. It nearly gave him a heart attack as he was wrenched awake to find her wrapped around him with her face buried in his neck.

"I'm sorry, Bruce, I'm sorry… It was mean and horrible and bad of me. And I was so afraid. I thought I had lost you. Please forgive me. I promise I won't leave you again, ever. I promise, I promise," she sobbed into his fur.

Unseen and undetected by Daisy, a small wiry man stood in the shelter of the trees watching as she threw herself on Bruce. He nodded to himself in approval and then there was the whisper of a breeze, and he was gone.

"*Well,*" Bruce thought, "*after that, I have to forgive you. But now you know how I felt when you weren't there and I thought you had gone forever.*"

"Do you really, truly forgive me, Bruce?"

"*Well, of course I do. How could I not when I love you so much?*"

"I love you too, Bruce. I don't suppose I knew how much until now," she said and kissed him on the nose.

"Blurg, yuk. That's worse than me licking you in the morning."

"OK," laughed Daisy. "Let's go. I want to show you something."

She stood up and pulled him to his feet. Holding on to his collar, she launched.

"What's that?" he thought, looking up.

"Oh that," explained Daisy, "that's a Cathedral,"

"Where are we?"

"Well," said Daisy, "Mum said you had sent me to Coventry, but I thought it would be much nicer if we could go there together."

Chapter Nineteen
Grandma's Broke

Daisy awoke gasping for breath and feeling decidedly flattened, but it only took her a few moments to realise that she was breathing in copious amounts of dog hair and that several large limbs were draped across her.

"Hey Bruce," she gasped, "I give in. I surrender."

"*Whoops, sorry,*" thought Bruce, wriggling off. "*I just wanted to be close.*"

"Well," said Daisy, "you'll be sorry when you wake up lying on a corpse."

"*Hey, that Coventry was a nice place. Can we go back again sometime?*"

"Not if I'm a corpse we won't."

"*OK, I'll try not to squash you too much in future.*"

"Not going anywhere today though because it's Grandma's day to ring us up. So," continued Daisy, "remove your large body from my small bed and let me get up."

Bruce jumped off the bed, gave a mighty shake from head to toe and then sat in the corner, well clear of the auto-clean that was about to start.

No more than two seconds later, washed and dressed, she and Bruce emerged from her bedroom and made their way downstairs to the kitchen for breakfast. Daisy climbed onto her chair at the table and Bruce buried his nose in the bowlful of dog biscuits that Marjorie placed on the floor for him.

"Hi Mum, Grandma is ringing today, isn't she?"

"Yes dear," said Marjorie, placing toast and cereal in front of Daisy. "Hey Bruce, do you want some tea to go with that biscuit?"

Bruce looked at his water bowl, sniffed at the smell of tea and said, "Woof."

Marjorie poured tea into a large mug, added milk and sugar, before emptying the water from his bowl and tipping the mug full of tea into it. Bruce attacked it with enthusiasm, totally ignoring the fact that it was hot, and slurped down great mouthfuls. He didn't like coffee very much, but he really was quite partial to a good bowl of tea.

After breakfast, Daisy and Bruce stayed around the house, eagerly awaiting the call from George's mother, but as the day progressed, everyone became more and more worried when the call didn't come. It was apparent that something was amiss as it was well into night time in Hawaii, and up until now, she had never missed a call.

"I shall phone her," said Marjorie eventually and picked up the phone to make the call. But a few minutes later, it became obvious that no one was answering.

"I know," she said. "I've got her neighbour's number, so I'll ring her. If there is no joy there, then we'll have to ring your dad at work."

Again she dialled, and spoke briefly into the phone, giving her identity and asking whether Millicent Daisy Weal was OK. She listened for a moment, said, "thank you for your help," and replaced the receiver.

"Apparently, she went for a walk this morning and hasn't been seen since, Daisy," said Marjorie. "The lady next door is now also worried and intends to call the police. I shall have to ring George."

It seemed like hours before George rushed in through the door, though in fact it could not have been more than thirty minutes. He immediately assumed control of the situation, much to his wife's and Daisy's relief.

"There's bound to be a rational explanation," he insisted. "She's probably gone to visit friends and forgotten what the time is. She is eighty-five after all. We'll all relax, have a cup of tea and wait for news from the authorities in Hawaii."

Marjorie made a pot of tea, poured them each a cup, sat down, then got up, added milk to the tea, then walked around the table, sat down again, then got up and sat down.

"I'm really worried, George," she said, "and afraid. She's an old lady. Something must have happened. She wouldn't forget to ring, and she wouldn't be out until this time of night."

"I agree, love," replied George. "I'm worried too, but what can we do?"

"Maybe," suggested Daisy quietly, "I could go and look."

Both George and Marjorie turned to look at Daisy, surprise and a glimmer of hope in their faces. It was George who spoke first.

"Would you, Daisy? I don't have any worries about you being safe, because I know you would be. But someone has to stay here though, in case anyone phones. Your mum and I need to be together, so you'd have to go alone."

"I won't be alone, Dad," said Daisy. "I'll have Bruce with me."

"It's night time there, Daisy," said Marjorie, "so make sure you are wrapped up well, and let me make you a couple of bread rolls to take along."

George left the room and returned a couple of minutes later with a photograph that he passed to Daisy.

"That's the latest picture we have of your gran. It was taken last year, so she shouldn't have changed much since then; just in case though, here's her address."

Daisy quickly went upstairs and returned with her small backpack. She put the picture, the address, the rolls Marjorie had prepared and the last-minute can of Pepsi Cola that George handed her into it, then hoisted it onto her back. She turned to call Bruce, only to find that he was already sitting next to her, waiting expectantly.

"See you later, Mum, Dad. Are you ready, Bruce?"

Bruce didn't even bother to think, just said 'Woof' and there was a loud 'pop' as they both vanished.

On Ala Moana Boulevard, near Waikiki in Hawaii, not far from the Ala Moana Shopping Centre, and also quite near to number 1508, is a large apartment block. In the shadows of its carpark, there was a sudden gust of air as a small nine-year-old girl and a large Boxer dog suddenly appeared. The Boxer promptly fell on his nose.

"I think our wittle Brucie has learning difficulties," said Daisy, in mock baby talk.

"*Shuddup*," replied Bruce, standing up unsteadily. "*I'll be alright in a minute.*"

"This is the right building, I think," said Daisy. "We need to go up to the third floor, but we have to remember that the bottom floor is number one here, and not the ground floor like at home. There's the main entrance," she continued. "I'm sure there'll be a lift."

As they walked towards the door, a small wiry man came out. He lifted a hand in a wave, smiled at Daisy and then simply faded away down the road. He didn't disappear, but literally faded out of existence as he walked. Daisy tried to sense him, but it was as if no one had ever been there, so she shrugged her shoulders and continued towards the entrance.

They pushed through the doors into a small lobby that had some stairs going upwards in the corner and two stainless steel doors marked 'Elevator' in the centre.

"There it is," she said, and walked over to the doors to push the calling button. The lift was already on their floor, so the doors slid quietly apart. Daisy and Bruce moved inside the doors and Daisy pressed the button for the third floor. The doors slid closed and the lift moved upwards with some speed, judging by the acceleration that pressed them downwards as the lift ascended. It stopped at the third floor with a jerk and the doors slid open.

"That's the one," said Daisy, pointing to a door down the corridor. They hurried to it and Daisy pressed the doorbell. A couple of seconds later, they heard footsteps and the door opened.

"Good grief...Daisy. What are you doing here at this time of night?" asked Candy-Anne. "Oh, never mind that, come on in and meet my mum and dad."

Introductions were completed with Bruce meeting Candy-Anne for the first time. At first, she was a little wary of him until he went up to her and laid his head in her lap. Daisy said hello to Candy-Anne's parents, and then the questions started.

"Whoa," said Daisy, "I'll explain but you won't believe me, so I'll have to show you. But let me tell you why I am here first."

The explanations were completed in about fifteen minutes, with Candy-Anne's parents looking at her in plain disbelief. Candy-Anne, however, did not seem so surprised.

"I never did believe the tale about the Hilton in New York," she said, "and I've been wondering ever since… OK, so show me."

There was a 'pop' and Daisy disappeared. The front doorbell rang and Candy-Anne went to let her back in. Candy-Anne's parents sat wide-eyed in silence, until her father said, "Well, OK, so now I believe it, but if anyone asks, I've seen nothing."

"Right," said Candy-Anne. "Now that you've told me where your grandma lives, I know that area. Not far from the houses, there's a pretty wild place, lots of trees and bushes, easy to get lost there and not easy to find anything. No one usually leaves the path because of that. There are also some pretty steep places. Perhaps we should start there?"

"Show me a picture with your mind," said Daisy, "and then hold my hand. Come on, Bruce, stay close."

Candy-Anne took hold of Daisy's hand and let her mind remember what the place was like the last time she was there. She closed her eyes. She felt a sharp twisting jerk and opened her eyes to darkness and trees and bushes next to the path they were on. Bruce lifted himself back to his feet and his thoughts were petulant, "*Yeh, yeh, I know, learning problems.*"

"Over there," said Candy-Anne, pointing, "see how it slopes down from the path."

"Bruce," said Daisy, "I can sense little thoughts that way, but it's now up to you."

"*Righto,*" thought Bruce and disappeared into the bushes.

Loud rustlings were heard for five minutes or so, and then a 'woof' followed by a faint voice, which said, "My, you're a big doggy. Well, if'n you've a mind to eat me, then I suppose you'd better get to it. I can't move so I aint' goin' nowhere. Mind you, I've got this 'ere big stick, so it ain't gonna be easy."

"*Well, there's this little woman down here all messed up,*" thought Bruce, "*thinks I want to eat her, but she looks too tough for that though. I'll stay here with her while you get help, because you won't be able to get down here without some rope. There are too many trees and bushes for you to use your normal method.*"

"Oh, then you ain't so tough. Perhaps you'll be right good company for me for a while," said the voice as Bruce lay down beside her.

"Grandma Millicent," shouted Daisy, accepting Bruce's word that teleportation was not an option, "is that you?"

"Dunno about the grandma, but my name most surely is Millicent...well, it is until I expire if someone don't get me out of here right quick."

"I've got my cell so I'll phone for help," said Candy-Anne.

"Who is that else up there with you?" asked the weak voice of Millicent. "For that matter, who are you to be callin' me grandma?"

"It's my friend, Candy-Anne, and she is phoning for help," shouted Daisy, "and I can call you Grandma because you are Millicent Daisy Weal, and I am your granddaughter Daisy Weal."

"And I've done died and gone to heaven," replied Millicent sarcastically, "and this 'ere dog is the Angel Gabriel."

Then they could hear the sounds of sirens in the distance, getting closer all the time.

"They'll be here soon," said Candy-Anne to Daisy. "It would be better if you weren't. Do you think Bruce could pretend to be mine?"

"Yes, he will," said Daisy, mentally passing the instructions on to Bruce. "I'll go and wait with your parents."

So Daisy disappeared to Candy-Anne's apartment just as the fire tenders, police and ambulance arrived. Millicent was eventually brought up gently on a stretcher. Candy-Anne was only questioned briefly, because Bruce attached himself to her and would not leave her side. He managed a few rumblings in his throat if anyone got too close to her, so the various law agencies decided she was an innocent bystander who, by coincidence, was becoming the heroine of the day.

Millicent looked oddly at Candy-Anne and let her gaze sweep around, but said nothing as she was hustled into an ambulance and whisked away.

Daisy returned home with the good news, though no one was prepared to declare it good until they knew for sure what Millicent's injuries were. She had brought an invitation from Candy-Anne's parents, inviting George and Marjorie to stay with them for as long as it took for Millicent to get well again. So bags were quickly thrown together and Daisy transported her parents, one at a time, back to Hawaii.

A couple of days later, they were able to visit Millicent in the hospital and were relieved but also still worried, because of Millicent's age, that the extent of her injuries was a single broken leg and a multitude of cuts and bruises.

Millicent looked at Daisy. "So y're the young'n as found me?"

"Yes Grandma, but what were you doing there in the first place?"

"No place for a young'n to be questionin' their olders," she said, then smiled. "Seein' though as I'm powerful glad t' see y'all, an y did rightly save me, I'll tell y. Well, more like, I'll tell m'boy, but first come'n give your grandma a hug."

She paused to take a breath, and Daisy took the opportunity to wrap her arms around her in a bear hug, and say, "Hi Grandma."

"Hi there yrself, Daisy Weal."

"Now George, it's like this. M' husband didn't 'ave as much as'n we thought when he up'n died them ten years back, an 'spite what'n I thought, the house ain't mine. So I was takin' a walk to run it through m' mind, when wump—I fell down this 'ere big hole, and 'ere I am."

"Never mind, Mum," said George, looking at Marjorie. She gave a slight nod of her head and he continued, "You can come to England and live with us."

"Y' know, George," she said, "I'd like that a much, 'n I could at least spend some time with m'granddaughter," she continued, "but I don't rightly think I could fly that far, at'n my age."

"No worries," said George, "Daisy will have us there in a tick."

Millicent looked at George, then Marjorie and then Daisy, before she said softly, "You know, I really do believe that she could." And all trace of her really weird accent was gone. Suddenly, she looked down at her plastered leg, giggled and said, "Well, you could say that I really am broke in more ways than one, couldn't you?"

Chapter Twenty
Making Things Right (1)

It was a couple of days before Daisy's tenth birthday when she awoke, with a feeling of determination, to find Bruce's nose in her ear and his leg around her neck. *Well, I suppose it's better than squashing*, she thought and wriggled out from under him.

"Hey Bruce, wake up lazy, we have a lot to do today. First, it's off to the shops with Mum and then we have a lot of things to put right."

"*Why?*" grumbled a still sleepy Bruce, "*what's happened?*"

"I'm nearly ten. It's time I grew up and made my mistakes right. I thought about it a couple of times, but I wasn't sure I was able…but I'm pretty sure I can now."

"*OK, wake me up when you've finished.*"

"Is it alright then if I do the room around—"

Before she could finish the sentence, Bruce was wide awake and sitting in his corner as far away from any activity as he could get.

"*A cruel child you are, Daisy Weal.*"

"Well, at least it got a certain very lazy dog off my bed. Before I get this place sorted, let's go and ask Mum when she's going into the shops." She paused. "Hey, I wonder if Grandma wants anything?"

Millicent Daisy Weal was in what had been the spare bedroom just down the hall. Her leg was now in a walking plaster and various healing cuts and bruises were still evident, so for a while yet, she would be staying around the house. As George had explained, Millicent was quite an old lady and things that would heal very quickly on Daisy, would take much longer with her.

She was at least able to hobble about on crutches and in three or four weeks, she should be able to get out and about. In the meantime, a Community Nurse popped in to check up on her every couple of days.

Daisy had considered speeding things up a bit, but she was not confident enough yet to take any chances. One day, when she had learnt enough about the workings of the human body—maybe, but not yet.

She knocked on Millicent's door and was greeted by, "Come in, Daisy."

She opened the door and replied, "How did you know it was me, Grandma?"

"Magic," replied Millicent.

"Don't be silly," retorted Daisy, "there is no such thing."

"Well then, tell me, oh granddaughter of mine, exactly what is it that *you* do?"

"I don't know, Grandma," said Daisy, "but it's not magic, because I don't use spells, and potions and things and," she grinned, "I haven't got a broom, or a cauldron, and Bruce could hardly be called a familiar."

"Familiar?" asked Millicent.

"Let's see if I can get the quote right," said Daisy. "I read up about it in the library, and this book said *'familiars were supernatural entities that were believed to assist witches and cunning folk in their practice of magic'*. They usually took the form of cats or birds, it said. But my way, I was told once, is that I 'manipulate the atomic structure of matter', whatever that means."

"Ah right!" said Millicent, looking at a very patient Bruce, with his tongue hanging out, sitting next to Daisy. "Nope, I don't think we can describe him as a familiar, but atomic structure or not, I think it's magic."

"Whatever you say, Gran," grinned Daisy, "but Mum and I are going into town; is there anything you want?"

"Oh rather," declared Millicent. "I'm afraid I have a weakness for wine gums."

"Righto then, wine gums it is," said Daisy, opening the door. "Come on, Bruce, you go down and get your breakfast, and I'll fix our room and get dressed."

Then she stopped and turned to face her grandmother again.

"I am curious, Grandma; what exactly happened to that really weird accent that you had when we first met?"

"Oh that!" laughed Millicent. "Well, it was a sort of defence mechanism when I found myself alone in a foreign country. I thought it would make me look quaint and vulnerable, and keep me safe. Stupid really, never was in any danger, but it got to be a habit until I realised I was coming home."

Bruce loped off downstairs while Daisy leaned over, kissed Millicent's cheek and then went back into her bedroom. She emerged immediately as if she had forgotten something, but fully dressed and obviously ready to start the day. A few seconds later, she joined Bruce in the kitchen. Marjorie was already there and in the process of filling Bruce's bowl with tea, but she looked up as Daisy entered.

"Morning, Daisy," she said. "I see you are ready for the shops. Not yet though, breakfast first."

As Daisy was about to sit down, she felt a sudden searing pain as if thousands of needles had just passed through her and at the same time, a violent tremor shook the house. It only lasted for a moment, but a cup jumped off the table and would have smashed had it not been for a quick thought from Daisy, which stopped it an inch from the floor. She quickly raised it back to the table and found she was sweating and her head hurt. She looked down at her fingers, which wouldn't stop trembling as if they had a life of their own.

"It's OK, Daisy," said Marjorie, who had noticed the effect on her daughter and quickly moved to comfort her, "it's only a small earthquake. We don't get many of that size in England, but sometimes it happens."

"I know, Mum," said Daisy. "I'm OK, just a bit shocked."

She said no more, but she knew that it was no earthquake. She had felt this before. Someone had created a reality shift and she felt a cold chill as she imagined that somewhere out there could be another person with the same powers that she had.

"*Please*," silently went through her mind, "*please make them responsible people.*"

After that, breakfast was finished in record time and pots, pans and plates were washed, dried and put away. Marjorie shouted upstairs to Millicent to say that they were going, and then they quickly left the house just in time to wave down a passing bus. It was quite against the bus company rules as there was no bus stop outside, but it stopped anyway and picked them up. When they arrived at the town centre, Daisy insisted that they go immediately to a sweet shop and buy Millicent's wine gums before they were forgotten. Then they made a whirlwind trip around the shops before stopping at a local café for a drink.

As they sat down, Daisy noticed a man who was sitting a few tables away and immediately recognised him as the ex-MI6 agent with the fat backside whose surveillance job she had managed to mess up. She wondered what he might be doing now, since the article that George had read out about the fiasco of the Russian spy had said that he had been fired.

"Hang on, Mum. I'll just be a minute. I need to talk to that man."

"Fine, dear," said Marjorie. "Don't be long, I'll get the tea."

Daisy went across the café to the ex-agent's table and said, "Excuse me, sir, I just wondered where your friend was?"

"Hey there, hello," he said jovially. "I know you, you're that little girl who got me promoted."

"Pardon?" said Daisy, totally confused.

"What's this about a friend?" he asked. "That day you helped me catch that Russian spy, there was only me and you. You ran around and locked the door so that she couldn't get away, and I managed to get handcuffs on her before the police arrived. Don't you remember?"

Discretion here, thought Daisy, *the man's gone nuts.* but aloud, she said, "Yes sir, I do. I must be thinking about something else. It is nice to meet you again, but I have to go now, as my mother is waiting over there." She pointed and then walked back across the café.

"Mum," she said, "do you remember that problem with the two MI6 agents?"

"Two?" asked Marjorie. "As I remember it, there was only one and he got promoted because he was the hero of the day, capturing that Russian spy. You dad read it out in the paper."

So that's what the reality shift did, thought Daisy. *Someone is messing with me. I think that man I keep seeing has something to do with this. But still, look on the bright side, that's one problem he's fixed for me.*

They caught the next bus home and Daisy ran into Millicent's bedroom, waving the bags of wine gums.

"We managed to get you some," she said cheerfully.

"Careful where you wave them," said Millicent, "you'll have someone's eye out."

"They're only wine gums, Gran, soft ones at that," said Daisy, piling more than was reasonably good for Millicent onto her bed.

"See you later. I'm off to my bedroom to read."

It's really odd how grandmas always think you can accidently extract eyes with the strangest objects, thought Daisy as she made her way to her own room.

○○●○○

Daisy sat on her bed, with one arm around Bruce and appeared to be off in a world of her own. Which in a way she was, for her mind was not there, but was moving outwards and searching for a little dog called Andrew. He should have been in the kennels for stray dogs, where he had been placed when he had been found in the police cell, but he wasn't. She became anxious, because she knew it wasn't right to leave him as a dog and she needed to reverse that before he lost his mind altogether. Once she had managed to do that, she was certain that he would be immediately recognised and sent back to prison where he belonged. His punishment would then rightly continue for the attempted bank robbery. So when she couldn't find him in the kennels, she broadened her search for the little dog.

She didn't find him. But after a while, to her surprise, she did manage to find a certain bank robber called Andrew Martin in a cell in jail. For a while, she watched him, and then noticed that he had taken up painting. But all he seemed to be painting were pictures of a small spaniel, on which he carefully painted the title 'Andrew'. She had to admit that they were really quite good. He was right where the law said he should be, Daisy decided, and judging from his current hobby, he might just be a much better person when he finally got out.

This reality shift was bigger than I thought. That's another thing that I didn't have to do, but now I have to see to Aunt Harriet. No. On second thoughts, I think that can wait for tomorrow.

Chapter Twenty-One
Making Things Right (2)

She knew she was going to be busy when she awoke the following day, but judging from yesterday's events, she had an uneasy feeling that all might not be as she was expecting it to be. She knew that she had to tell her mother what had happened and what she was trying to do, because having a daughter sitting on her bed all day in a trance might just worry her a little. So she carried out her morning ritual in the twinkling of an eye, being careful to avoid the corner where Bruce was taking refuge. Then she breezed down the stairs to breakfast, with him being careful not to allow his rear end to overtake as he followed.

"Hi Mum," she said, "I have things to tell, and confessions to make."

"Oh dear," said her mother, a worried expression appearing on her face. "Nothing of a cataclysmic nature, I hope?"

"Well, tell me what 'cataclysmic' means," replied Daisy, "and I'll tell you whether I did it."

"Cataclysmic," said Marjorie, "in your case, would be the imminent end of life as we know it."

"Oh no," said Daisy, "nothing like that; more the reverse really."

"Ah!" said Marjorie with a sigh of relief. "Do tell, I'm all ears."

"Well, you're not really, but I'm sure it could be arranged if required."

"What could be arranged?" asked a confused Marjorie.

"Oh, to make you all ears, what else?"

"Oh, shut up, Daisy, and make your confession," sighed Marjorie as she sat down at the table.

So Daisy explained, mostly what her mother already knew or suspected, and then went on to talk about the wiry man and her suspicions about him. She explained how she had decided that it was time to correct her mistakes and what she had found when she had tried. She explained about reality shifting and how it apparently affected everyone, including her mother, but not her. Then she finished off by explaining how reality had been affected in this particular instance, and what it had been before the shift.

"So," she finished, "I will be in my room all day to see if I can fix what's left or, I suppose, discover that it's already been fixed for me."

Marjorie just sat and looked at her for what seemed like an age but in reality was only a couple of minutes, and then said, "Your life is so complicated, Daisy, and you are only ten. How do you cope?"

"Sometimes it's hard," said Daisy thoughtfully, "then it occurs to me that my wiry gentleman may actually be looking out for me and I do feel a lot better."

She finished her breakfast and then made her way to her room, armed with her mother's promise to see that she wasn't disturbed. Marjorie had stood in front of Bruce, wagging her finger, charging him with the task of sitting with

Daisy to make sure any problems were communicated promptly.

"*I only got a couple of words of that,*" thought Bruce. "*Haven't you told her I only understand you?*"

Daisy repeated everything Marjorie had said into Bruce's mind and assured him that she had explained to her mother who, apparently, automatically expected Daisy to pass on the message.

Her thoughts winged her off across the Atlantic to Canada where, not knowing exactly where Harriet was being kept, she sent out her thoughts to policemen, and then court officials, to find the specific place of detention that Harriet was being kept in. Once she had it located, she moved towards Aunt Harriet's presence, though she was temporarily confused, because the thoughts she found were quiet, humbled and of a much nicer nature than she had grown to expect.

She arrived just in time to witness a tall and strikingly beautiful lady being released from detention. A very worried-looking official was saying that he did not know what idiot in Customs could not see that she was obviously the person on her passport. Could she ever forgive them for such a ridiculous mistake, and if she felt it necessary to sue, would she please not mention his name?

A hastily convened court had come to the conclusion that there had been a serious miscarriage of justice and had ordered her immediate release. An investigation was being launched to determine why her photograph, fingerprints and DNA did not match those that had been taken at the time of her arrest. Along with the release instructions, came an abject apology from the court.

Aunt Harriet looked back into the bare room that she had been kept in and without the slightest hint of sarcasm in her voice, said, "Well, under the circumstances, the accommodations were fine and I've had absolutely no trouble at all. So I've no intention of suing, as the whole thing has obviously been an honestly made mistake. Now if you will excuse me," she added, "I have an apology to make to my sister, and a new trip to England to arrange so that I can try at least, to make my niece love me."

Well, that seems to have done her good, though really she shouldn't be back to normal yet. But she's better than normal, so let's not worry. Let's move on.

The Swain boys were a successful operation, she thought, *as was Jimmie, and the milkman came to no harm and can't remember anything, so I can forget him. I can stop the green faces from happening again, and they didn't cause any real problems anyway, only a great deal of good. So then, it's off to find the postman.*

●●●●●

In a small block of apartments, in a small back street, quite a way from the town centre of Bishop's Ashton, a medium-built and quite miserable man was carefully shaving his green face. He hadn't been out for weeks, because he was too embarrassed by the laughter he encountered when he did. He seemed to be the last one, had finally given up trying to find his own special piece of rubbish and was becoming resigned to a lifetime of ridicule. It had only been a chewing gum wrapper after all, and he had only thrown it into a gully beside the road.

Why did he deserve this punishment? His wife had left him, saying he should have realised that no matter how small it was, all rubbish mattered, and she had no intention of living with an idiot, especially an idiot with long yellow ears.

As it happens, Daisy didn't know he existed. She didn't know everything, couldn't know everything. The world is too big a place, and he was only one man. Because she thought it was over, having not seen a green face in ages, she didn't send out the thought that would have reversed it. So it certainly looked as if he would be remaining green, with really beautiful long yellow ears, for many, many years to come.

Fortunately for him, there was a small wiry individual who did know everything. So one day, a knock on his door caused him to hastily pull a hat over those ears before he answered it.

"Mr Franks?" asked the small and wiry man who stood there, "Mr Cedric Franks?"

"Yes, that's me," he said.

"You've got something that you don't need any more. I've come to remove it." Then he turned and walked away.

"How odd," said Cedric to the empty corridor and closed his front door. As he turned away from the door, he noticed a crumpled-up chewing gum wrapper next to the telephone. Without thinking, he picked it up and dropped it into the waste bin next to the hall stand. As he looked up from the bin, he caught a glimpse of his face in the hall mirror and stopped dead. His own normal, recently clean-shaven face looked back at him. Frantically, he ripped off the hat and was greeted by the sight of two very normal ears adorning the sides of his head. He stood and stared for a while, then reached for his coat and said, "I think it's time to go down to the pub for a drink."

●●●●●

Daisy, having decided to find the postman, swiftly glided off to the post office, pretty sure that morning postal rounds were complete by this time, as it was now early afternoon. Positioned herself carefully, she observed the activity of the sorting office and had just spotted Alfred, when one of his colleagues asked, "Hey Alf, are you going anywhere nice for your break this year?"

"Well, I hope so," said Alfred. "I've booked a couple of weeks for me and the family in some place called Benidorm in Spain. Thought I'd look up some ancestors and," he added, "get a bit of sun, sand and sea air."

"Sounds good. Have you been to Spain before?"

"No, I haven't, but the brochure looks good and it's pretty cheap this time of year."

This is saving me a job, thought Daisy, *but it is also becoming very irritating.*

●●●●●

"OK, Mark and Angela Frogget, let's see if I can get to you before Mr Wiry does."

Her mind arrived at the Psychiatric Unit, just in time to see cases being piled into a waiting taxi and a white-coated man holding the Unit door open so that Mark and Angela could come out.

"It seems," he was saying, "that your lawyer has argued that nothing in your pamphlets, or advertisements, actually said you were witches, or even promised that you would actually teach working spells. We've also been back over the transcripts of the court and our consultations and it seems that you never ever claimed to be witches."

"Of course, we didn't," said Mark and Angela together. Quite quick on the uptake, they were. "We were just providing realistic training for would-be entertainers and people interested in the history of witchcraft."

"Well, we deeply apologise, Mr and Mrs Frogget, and solicitors will be in touch with you shortly to discuss compensation." He continued, "Arrangements have been made for Michael to be returned to you this afternoon. Odd though, after he was told, he disappeared. Took us ages to find him, he never did explain how he got locked in the broom cupboard."

"Are you sure he can't stay with the foster parents?" asked Mark.

"Be quiet, Mark," said Angela.

Oh well, thought Daisy, *only a couple to go, but I'm tired so that's for tomorrow.*

Chapter Twenty-Two
Loose Ends

Yesterday had taken a lot more out of Daisy than she had expected, so it was Bruce who woke up first and then began to worry when he could not rouse her. In the end, he used his ultimate weapon, full face lick, followed by the nose in the ear ploy. A spluttering Daisy came to life, arms waving and body rolling away from the assault.

"What are you doing, Bruce?" she gasped. "Are you trying to drown me?"

"*You wouldn't wake up,*" thought Bruce. "*I got worried.*"

She could sense the easing panic in him so, relenting, she put her arms around his neck.

"Thanks Bruce," she said. "I got really tired after that out of body stuff yesterday. It seems to take more out of me than anything else."

"*You're welcome,*" thought Bruce. "*Hurry up, I'm hungry.*"

Over breakfast, she brought her mother and a quite intrigued George up to date with progress, but left out the fact that it was more tiring than she expected. *Just a couple more things*, she thought, *and then I can take some time to recharge.*

After breakfast, she said goodbye to her father as he left for work, standing on tiptoe to kiss his cheek, and then helped her mother clear the breakfast things and load the dishwasher. A few minutes later, she excused herself and returned to her room. *Just these last few loose ends and then I'm done*, she thought.

The visit to the golf course took a lot less time than Daisy had anticipated. For as soon as she slid into the clubhouse, she saw that the little area that had been set up to commemorate the exploits of one George Weal, Club Champion, was not there anymore. So she returned to her body in her bedroom.

"I must phone Dad at work, Bruce," she said.

"*Ah, you're back,*" he observed. "*Better clear it with your mum first.*"

"Come on then," she said and headed out of the bedroom and down the stairs.

"Mum, I need to phone Dad to ask him some questions," she said. "Important, to do with the reality shift, have you got his number?"

"Of course, dear." Marjorie scribbled the number down on a piece of paper and handed it to Daisy. "He is at work, so don't keep him long."

"I won't," said Daisy, quickly lifting the phone and dialling the number.

"Hi Dad," she said when he answered. "I need to ask you a couple of things."

"Hi Daisy, ask away, I'm not too busy at the moment," said George.

"I'm writing an essay for school," she fibbed, "and I wanted to add something about the golf game that you took me and Bruce to."

"Oh yes, that was the one where I just managed to beat Cyril Foster by one stroke. He was such an arrogant idiot that he couldn't take to lose even by one, so he left the company and being next in line, I got his job."

"That's fine, Dad, thanks, that's all I wanted to know, see you at home later."

Always one step ahead, Mr Wiry, she thought, *let's see if you can keep it up.*

Back in her bedroom again, she soared over Brighton with the intention of removing all of the obstacles to the return of the Pavilion from the moon, but when she got there, she discovered that building work had already commenced. As she drifted around the half-finished building, she realised that it was in fact going to be an exact copy of the original. There was obviously nothing to be done, so she quietly thanked Brighton for the gift of her home on the moon and made a vow that she would always keep an eye on this seaside town, and if it ever needed anything in the future, then she would provide it.

Daisy began to picture a certain corner on a certain avenue in New York. When she had it clear in her mind, she gathered her thoughts and launched. She felt nothing and opened her eyes. She was still in her bedroom. She tried again and still nothing happened. Her brow furrowed in concentration and she reached out instead with only her thoughts, felt resistance, and found…nothing.

"And why not?" she asked into the silence around her.

"*Because there is no need,*" the soft thought came into her mind, "*there is nothing here that you have done wrong. That man got less than he deserved, but it is enough. The three little girls are safe because of you, and countless others have been spared what those little girls had to go through.*"

"What about Chuck, and his friends, and the Luna mission?" she asked.

"*Not a problem. You cannot retrieve the Pavilion and the mystery of its existence on the moon will intrigue the human race for a long time, as will the picture of a little girl waving from next to it. No harm was done. Chuck and his friends were saved from the re-entry disaster and are now doing just as they probably had wanted to do all their lives. In addition, they have you as a friend and are party to your secret, even though I suspect that they still don't really believe it. No,*" the thoughts continued, "*I think that problem is one best left alone.*"

"What about Grandma?" she asked.

"*That was not of your doing. It was a normal accident, and she is recovering nicely. Perhaps, in a way, it was fortunate; at least she now has a home where she is loved and appreciated, and can see her granddaughter whenever she wants to.*"

"You are the *Vana*, aren't you?" she asked, realising that she had probably always known.

"*Yes, we are*," came the reply.

Chapter Twenty-Three
Home

Daisy was at her usual place in the garden, a place where no one would notice if she was sitting still. She was idly playing with the sand in the sandpit, but without concentration. Physically she was there, but mentally she was zooming down through the Ngora Ngora crater in Tanzania. Racing with the Wildebeest and Zebras, then pretending to ride a Rhino, before zooming off to startle the Flamingos with her passing. It always surprised her that birds always seemed to sense a presence when she was near. But it did add to the fun. Then she was moving off towards the lake and the hippos, when suddenly her link broke and she was snapped back to the sandpit. Movement to her right attracted her and she turned.

A faint haze had appeared in the corner of the garden. Gradually, it was getting brighter until it was difficult to look at. A form appeared in the haze, but it could not be seen clearly. It was more of a fiery outline with the vague shape of a person. Then, the outline began to fade, and the shape solidified into a small wiry-looking man.

At least he has arms and legs, and I've seen him before, thought Daisy, somewhat reassured.

"Hello Daisy, we have come to take you home," came directly into her mind, and she recognised it as the ***Vana***.

"Well, that was a bit dramatic," she said aloud. "Every other time that I've seen you, you've just been there. Is this really what you look like then?"

"Not really," he replied in kind, "but we've used this form while we've been watching you and we thought our real form might frighten you."

"Not a lot can do that anymore," she replied, "but thanks for the consideration."

It was odd to be spoken to when in the past, it had always been thoughts. It felt quite different to the previous conversations. *OK then, this must be learning day*, she thought.

For a moment she was silent, as thoughts gathered and rushed through her head. She hesitated and then: "Where is this home that you think you're taking me to then?" she asked, remembering what he had said when he had appeared.

"Among the stars," came the reply. "You will be part of us. With us, you will be able to explore worlds more different and stranger than you can imagine."

"What are you?" asked Daisy, reverting to mind to mind.

"We think that we were formed at the same time as the Universe itself, and for a long time, there was no one else. We found that we had absolutely no way to expand, to become larger, and it became quite desperate when parts of us started to die. Those parts needed to be replaced because we were losing some power each time one was lost. So we developed a way to plant part of us into new races that were beginning to appear so that we could harvest them later,

make them part of us, make us whole again and survive. You are the first on this Planet and after observing you, we have great hopes for this place."

Daisy looked towards the house and realised that the **Vana** had made her mother a part of the conversation. She could see the tears flowing down Marjorie's face as she watched. Her heart went out to her mother and for the first time, she sent a thought, soft as eiderdown, into her mother's mind.

"It's alright, Mum, it will be alright."

She turned back to the small wiry man that was the presence of the **Vana**.

"That's all very well, but why would I want to come with you?"

This was unexpected and the **Vana** was clearly startled.

*"The whole Universe as a playground, who would not want that? As part of us, you will be able to visit Worlds where the sun shines every day, Worlds where darkness thrives, Worlds where the thunder from storms is always in the air, Worlds that have no people and Worlds where there are billions. With us, you could go to a World where volcanoes are in continual eruption and Worlds that are rolling grasslands. Worlds that are filled with water and Worlds where there is none. As part of the **Vana**, the beauty of the universe is your inheritance."* He paused. *"The power we have is limitless, and as part of us, then so it would be for you. You have already served a great purpose for us, by bringing the **Somethings** to our attention. You have a talent that we don't have, but one that we need."*

For a long time, she stared at him; then she reached out for him mentally. "*Come with me,*" she thought, and took him, and showed him. She showed him the Earth as she saw it. She showed him the oceans, and the beaches, and the deserts, and the mountains. She showed him the plains, and the valleys, and the volcanoes, and the ice flows in the Arctic. She showed him the snow, and the rain, and hurricanes, and tornadoes. Then she showed him the forests, and grass, and animals, and insects, and finally, she showed him the people.

"*Everything that you have told me about, I already have here. I don't need to go anywhere. Beside which, I have a mother and father who love me, not because of what I am, but despite what I am. This is not an old planet, and the people are not old. They make mistakes and at times they can be cruel, but there are a lot more times when they can be kind, tender and loving. They try, **Vana**, they try, and I am part of them. I am much more a part of this world and these people than I am of the **Vana**. Oh, I feel the **Vana** inside me and I feel that I am part of it. But I am me, an individual, and for me the only 'us' is the hands that I old, and the love that I receive. This is my home.*" There was no hesitation in her thoughts and they came straight and strong. "*And I'm staying here.*"

"*I suppose that trying to change your mind would be time wasted,*" they observed, and there was sadness in their thoughts.

"*Yes, I am already at Home.*"

"*We have tried to, but something in your human makeup prevents us from forcing you, and I suppose that it would be counter-productive if we could. It's not what we intended or wanted, so your decision has been noted and will be respected. We worry a little that we may have created something new, that there may be a uniqueness here that we have not seen elsewhere. So we will be watching you, and should you need us, we will be here. But until we know, you'll be the only one and we'll not use this planet again."*

A race of beings whose children were not really children, only part of something else, and precious only because they completed the whole, or a World where there were millions, all individual, all different and all the more precious for it.

"*Visit any time,*" smiled Daisy, "*but somehow, I don't think I will need you, because here, I am never alone.*"

"*Take care, Daisy Weal,*" they said. "*Your power is awesome, use it well.*"

Then the small wiry man, for the final time, vanished from the light in the corner of the garden. And gradually, as the breeze of his passing whispered, the light faded and was gone.

Daisy turned and looked, and saw that the light in her mother's face was brilliant and shining, and through the tears of joy, her radiant smile was there for the whole world to see.

The End

Excerpt from Book 2:
Daisy Weal and the Monster
Chapter One: The Invasion

In about nine months, Daisy would be eleven and was blossoming into quite the little lady. She was much too beautiful for a child of her age, and it was becoming apparent that when she reached her teens, there would be queues of young men prepared to do almost anything for just one glance of approval, or even the slightest nod of recognition, from her. She had not quite reached that stage yet; besides which, she always had a very large boxer dog walking beside her, and not far away, there would be Alfie.

Alfie was the same age as Daisy and at the moment was convinced that he was completely in love with her. At his age, he should have been playing football or rugby, but was so hopelessly smitten that he was rarely anywhere else but with her. His parents just thought he was being silly; after all, how could he possibly be in love at his age? He probably wasn't really, but even at ten, those huge green eyes had sucked him in and his soul was lost—if not forever, then for the moment at least—to one Daisy Weal.

This was the week that the world was invaded, but what was worse was that the whole thing was Daisy's own fault. However, she was not to know that until much later. It was quite a small invasion as invasions go, because there was only one being in the first wave.

I call it a first wave, even though it was only one being, because this one being was pretty huge and had forty-two arms, forty-two legs and forty-two eyes. It did only have one mouth, but in that mouth were forty-two very sharp teeth and a large number of tongues. There may have been forty-two, who knows? I for one was not going in there to count, so the true number is anyone's guess.

Big, bold, terrifying and totally confused it was, as anything would be if it was only able to look in forty-two directions at once. Where it came from, things were different and there was no confusion, as each single way *was* forty-two directions. Oh, and I almost forgot, it was one hundred and forty-two-foot square, which, for those who know no better, is approximately 43 metres. He was also a male of his species.

He wasn't *actually* square, but if you were able to squash him into a cube, then that would be his size. It has to be admitted that he was a little overweight as, in accordance with the prevailing precedents, he should only have been 42 metres square. Unfortunately though, this monster was rather fonder of his food than most of his brethren and was consequently a little overweight.

I know that such a beast is impossible and its very presence flies in the face of known science. However, I suppose you could say that of the centipede, which I believe has far more legs that it is entitled to. But this monster not only had forty-two legs and arms, it was also a garish purple and red, with a yellow underside. Its red fingers, on black arms, matched perfectly with its bright red eyes, which made it look a lot like a cartoon character. If anything, its appearance was the more terrifying for it.

You could say that, with its arms and legs combined, it was an octagintapede; that's eighty legs in Latin, by the way, with an extra four tagged on for luck, but what made it more impossible was its head, which was literally covered with eyes. More peculiar though was its diet. It had tried a human shortly after arrival, but had spat it out before even taking a bite because it had tasted so awful. Then it had discovered road signs and proceeded to wander towards Bishop's Ashton, popping them into its mouth like lollipops on the way. But I am rambling, so let's get back to the story.

●○●○●

It started as quite a normal day, with Daisy being awoken by an impending feeling of doom, which turned out to be Bruce in suffocating mode.

I might have to sleep in a protecting field, she thought, *or I'll wake up as that corpse I promised this silly dog.*

"*Who are you calling a silly dog?*" asked a still half-asleep Bruce.

"You, you halfwit," said Daisy aloud. "You have to be more careful, you are really big and I am only little."

"*And that is my fault how?*" he asked.

"Your size is not your fault," retorted Daisy, "but how you use it, is."

She looked at him sternly. "Now get off the bed and let me clean up in here."

She brushed her teeth at the little wash basin beside the bed, delighting in the fact that she could do it without using her hands, and then went into the bathroom across the hall.

"You have ten seconds to get out," she shouted back over her shoulder, "before I wave me magic wand."

"*You don't have a magic wand,*" protested Bruce.

"Wanna bet?"

"*No,*" thought Bruce, making it to the safety of his corner in a single bound.

"Today," said Daisy as she returned from the bathroom, "I am going to wander around a few in-between places."

"*Probably be a disaster,*" said Bruce telepathically, and then, "*No probably about it. It will definitely be a disaster.*"

"You really are a harbinger of doom, aren't you?"

"*For a dog,*" he replied, "*I am pretty bright, but I would really like to know what a harbinger is.*"

Daisy reached for the dictionary that was in the bookcase beside the little wash basin and thumbed through it.

"Ah, here it is. It says, '*One that indicates or foreshadows what is to come; a forerunner*'. And that, in my opinion, is as clear as mud."

"*Well, I've been in ignorance up until now,*" he observed, "*so I don't suppose a bit longer will matter.*"

Daisy grinned as she led him downstairs.

"You and me both," she acknowledged.

Daisy wasn't in any hurry this morning as it was her school midterm holidays, and that made the weekend longer than normal. Revelling in the unaccustomed luxury, she took her time with breakfast, stretching it out for as long as she could. After her third cup of tea, she turned to her mother, who had been patiently reading the morning newspaper while she waited, and said, "I shall be wandering off today, but only in my head, of course. There are a few places I need to see."

"Yes dear," said Marjorie understandingly. "Where, the sand pit or the bedroom?"

"Bedroom, I think. The sky looks a bit thundery and as you know, I don't do wet," she replied.

"I can never understand why you don't stick up a virtual umbrella or something," said Marjorie.

"Because I keep forgetting to move it when I move myself," explained Daisy. "It's easier to avoid the stuff in the first place."

"OK then, I'll try not to disturb you, but I will let Grandma know when she gets up."

Daisy gave Bruce a mental nudge and then trotted up the stairs with him closely behind. Jumping up onto her bed, she settled herself comfortably with Bruce's head on her lap; closing her eyes, she immediately drifted off towards the nearest in-between place that was within sight. Suddenly, she was standing underneath the front arms of a…huge…something…and instinctively jumped away, as a head full of eyes and a massive mouth came towards her. All she could see was this purplish monster, with these really weird stripes, loads of arms, legs, eyes, teeth and a massive body.

In the blink of an eye, her mind was back in the bedroom, transferring her terror to her body, which started trembling almost uncontrollably. She had apparently jumped physically as well as mentally, because Bruce was in his safe corner, looking at her with wide eyes.

"*What happened? Are you OK?*"

"Er…yes, I think so," she said, her voice wobbling, but then a glint of amusement. "And you're going to protect me from that corner… Oh, my hero."

"*Well, I withdrew to this corner to consider my options,*" thought Bruce defensively.

"There was this massive *thing*… It was probably harmless, but one look and I was not hanging around to find out. What is worse is that I was only a thought and it *saw* me. It scared the living daylights out of me, but I'll be alright in a minute," she finished.

"*Huh!*" bragged Bruce. "*Just bring him here, and then we'll see what's what.*"

"Ha! He'd have glopped you in one bite," laughed Daisy, feeling much better.

Bruce showed his teeth in a mock snarl. "*Am I not big, fearsome and frightening?*"

"'Fraid not. You are just a big old softy," she said, going over to him and wrapping her arms around his neck, but then she paused and looking out of the window at the sky, she added, "And rain or no rain, I think we'll go play in the sand pit. I can always erect Mum's virtual umbrella and divert the wet stuff around us."

●○●○●

Back in a certain in-between place, the forty-two eyes noticed that where that little thing had appeared and then disappeared, there was a tiny place where he could see something else. It looked like a small rip in mid-air with light shining through that was no more than a few centimetres in length. The monster didn't know it, but it seemed that Daisy had been so startled that she had forgotten to close the door properly before she left. He peered closely at the rip and then reaching forward with a pair of arms, he started to prise it open. For a monster of his size, and with forty-two arms, it was easy. Very soon, he had made an opening that was big enough for him to squeeze through.

It is fortunate that in-between places and the real world do not have fixed relationships; otherwise, this would have been a very different story indeed. They do move about, so instead of the monster materialising next to Daisy on her bed, he popped into existence on the main road to Bishop's Ashton. Being in a different place, with different laws of physics, he quickly became confused because of the conflicting stories that all of his eyes were telling him. However, he did notice the cyclist who was trying to scramble away on hands and knees from where he had fallen from his bike, screaming at the top of his voice.

So, being suddenly very hungry, the monster grabbed the man with his closest pair of arms and then lifted him up to an eye. Looking the cyclist over for a second, he licked a great many tongues across his forty-two teeth and then popped the man into his mouth.

"Grrr! Yuk thut!" he said and spat the worst thing he had ever tasted out onto the ground. Then, spotting the man's bike, he picked that up and ate it instead. The man had tasted so awful on several of his tongues that he hadn't even been able to take a bite, but had reflexively spat him out instead. Thus, it was that a mortally terrified man, covered in monster slobber and screaming as though it was the end of the world, ran away as fast as his wobbling legs would take him.

"Mmm," said the monster, licking his lips with his whole load of tongues.

He then picked out the tyres and saddle from between his teeth with his first pair of arms and threw them away. The metal was delicious, but the leather and rubber were not his cup of tea at all. Looking around for more, one of his eyes spotted a speed limit sign, not that he knew it was a speed limit sign, but it seemed to be made of the same stuff as the bike, so a pair of arms plucked it from the ground and into the mouth. All forty-two eyes rolled in ecstasy at the taste. It was even better than the first thing he'd eaten, so the serious task of finding more of these delectable morsels began.

A soaking wet, gabbling man eventually waved down a passing police car and poured forth the most ridiculous and impossible story that the two officers had ever heard. They were about to arrest him for a variety of offences when, around a bend in the road, rambled the monster, happily munching road signs as he went. On went the sirens as the police driver executed a perfect handbrake turn, and with his foot hard down on the pedal, accelerated away towards Bishop's Ashton. His companion was on the radio, hysterically calling for police reinforcements, the army, the navy and the air force, and even a nuclear strike. Not that the latter was about to happen anytime soon but as no one believed him, it didn't matter anyway.

"The navy won't be a lot of good out here in the countryside," the driver said helpfully as he gunned the car down the narrow, winding country road at a suicidal 140mph.

Screeching to a halt in front of the police station, they were immediately surrounded by their colleagues and taken into custody on suspicion of being drunk. After being breathalysed and found to have no alcohol in their blood, they were interrogated extensively, but eventually released back to duty, pending the review of the police car's on-board camera.

By now, other reports corroborating the two officers' stories were flooding in and these were soon confirmed by the scenes captured by the car's camera. In the end, the sergeant had to order everyone back to work as they crowded around the screen.

Some very old wartime emergency procedures were put into action and the civil defence was alerted. At first, they thought it was a joke until the online pictures started to arrive, at which point they wasted no time in calling in the army, who in turn called the air force. The media somehow got wind of something momentous and news teams from the BBC, ITV, Sky, CNN and even Al Jazeera were soon converging on the source of the story. Within minutes, newsflashes started to appear on television and crowds of people with more curiosity than sense began to arrive in Bishop's Ashton. It was early days yet for pictures, but soon cameras would be on site. Until then, graphic descriptions from obviously disbelieving newsreaders saturated the airwaves.

The first real pictures came in via the air force, who had sent a high-speed, low-level, unmanned reconnaissance drone. A bit too low really as the aircraft produced, but only briefly, some wonderful pictures of a magnificent set of teeth as it flew straight into the monster's mouth. Almost instantly, however, these were shown on television and that's when Daisy saw them.

"Oh my God," she said. "Oh Mum, I think I let it out."

"Well, perhaps," said Marjorie, who tended to be perfectly calm in even the most difficult of circumstances, "you had better get him back home, before he does some real damage."

Daisy had no time for running so she zoomed up the stairs without touching them and into her bedroom. Bruce, not having the same luxury, took the flight three at a time and managed to arrive closely behind her, but it seemed like only a second before they both came back out again and down the stairs.

By now, TV cameras were on site, and the first shaky pictures began to be shown to accompany the almost hysterical commentary. Daisy and Marjorie pulled their chairs closer to the television, leaning forwards to see as much as they could.

"I can't, Mum. I've locked on to where he's from, but I need to be much closer and he needs to keep still. He's much too big and too alive. If he was a building, I wouldn't have a problem."

"You can't get closer, it's too dangerous. Royal Air Force planes are probably going to be bombing him soon, if the army doesn't shell him to death first. Let's just watch and see what happens."

"But I can't let them kill him, Mum, I just can't!"

Tanks rolled up the road from manoeuvres that had been taking place in an area not too far from Bishop's Ashton, and practice ammunition had been hastily changed for the real stuff. As soon as the first tank came into view of the monster, it swivelled its gun and let rip without warning. The monster did no more than place its mouth in the line of fire and gulp down the shell, with much lip smacking and tongues licking. The tank fired again, but the monster simply caught the shell in one of its arms and bit the end off.

"I'm not sure you'll have to worry about him being killed," observed Marjorie, "he seems to be holding his own quite well."

By this time, the tanks behind the first one had fanned out into the fields, brought their guns to bear and fired together, but the monster had a lot of arms and was beginning to appreciate this sudden feast that was being thrown at him. He moved forward, picked up the first tank, broke off the top and shook out the very nasty-tasting things inside, then took a mighty bite, then another, before shoving the remainder into its mouth to chew. The remaining tank crews had seen enough and hastily fled, squeezing every ounce of speed that they could out of their tanks. Later, it would be described as a controlled, orderly and strategic withdrawal, but I saw it and I say they fled.

The first salvo of rockets and stream of cannon fire from the incoming ground attack aircraft streaked towards the monster. Most were caught, but some managed to strike it. The small intense bursts of light from the explosions appeared to be only a minor irritant and the 20mm cannon shells just seemed to bounce off. The aircraft were very careful to keep sufficient altitude to be out of reach of the monster, and after a couple of more ineffective attacks, they broke off and disappeared away to the west.

Obviously, nothing short of a nuclear strike was going to have any effect and no one in their right mind would authorise that on British soil and expect to remain un-lynched. A special meeting of COBRA was called, but other than leaving the threat level unchanged, it accomplished little. Events were moving so fast though that they overtook any decision-making processes, and the authorities were left as mere spectators to something that was completely out of their control.

Then, gasps of astonishment...

"What's that?" asked a cameraman, pointing towards the small figure that was walking slowly towards the monster.

"It looks like a little girl. I can't believe it...she'll be eaten...quick, keep your camera on her."

"Excuse me, sir, what's your name?" asked Daisy, looking up at the monster as he wiped the remains of tank from his lips. She realised he probably could not understand her, so she reinforced the message mind to mind.

"*Go away*," he said. "*I've tried you things and you don't taste nice, and anyway, what is this place? Everything is wrong, I can't see properly.*"

"Can you control all of your eyelids?" asked Daisy.

"*Yes, I can; why?*" he asked.

"Well, close all the others, but keep only two open in the front, like we have," she said, pointing to her own eyes.

The monster bent down and gazed into her face from only a few inches away, and the whole world held its breath. Then slowly, the eyes all over his head began to close and soon there were only two that gazed down sadly at Daisy.

"*Thanks, that's much better*," he said. "*My name is Bllrrsdle. Apart from all this good food, I don't like it here, but I can't find my way home.*"

"That's OK, Blursdel," she said, not quite getting the pronunciation right. "My name is Daisy Weal. I can send you home, but I think we should get you some food first. You stay here and I'll be back."

The monster sighed and settled down on forty-two haunches, folded forty-two arms, closed his mouth over forty-two teeth and the world let out a collective sigh of relief.

Daisy made her way to the first person in the crowd that looked official, and he immediately asked what she had done to pacify such a horrendous beast.

"Nothing really," she said and stretching the truth a little, continued, "He said he would go home if he could have some more of those things to eat that you have sticking up all over the place."

"What, road signs?" someone else of importance asked, then not waiting for an answer, said, "I'm sure we can find a few… Small price to pay."

It only took a little mental twisting from Daisy to prevent all of the awkward questions that people were dying to ask. There were, however, quite a few who later wondered why they had not asked them at the time.

Orders were given and trucks despatched to the local council yards, where new and old road signs that had been in storage were loaded, while other workmen began ripping up those on all the streets in Bishop's Ashton. Soon, several lorries loaded with signs rolled up to the monster and tipped them into the road in front of him. He smacked his lips again and began gathering them up into a lot of arms.

Daisy looked around, then selected a man out of the hundreds of people who were staring in terrified fascination at Bllrrsdle and walked up to him.

"May I borrow your belt, sir?" she asked.

Without taking his eyes from the monster, he removed his belt and handed it over, as if giving it to any little girl who asked for it was an everyday occurrence.

Belt in hand, she walked back to Bllrrsdle and wrapped it around a concrete lamppost, before securely fastening herself with it. The monster was happy with his arms full of road signs and sat still while Daisy sent him home. As he blinked out of existence, there was a massive 'crack' and a howling gale blew most of the onlookers off their feet, while one man whose trousers were around his ankles was blown into a bush. Daisy was lifted from her feet for a second, but the belt held and the wind died as the hole left by the huge, one-hundred-and-forty-two-foot creature was filled with air. Daisy made absolutely sure that the entrance was finally sealed properly, then untied herself and returned the belt to the onlooker, who was desperately trying to maintain his dignity as he struggled out of the bush.

"Love the underpants, by the way," she remarked. "What made you pick daisies?"

The man growled something and hastily retrieved his trousers before disappearing into the crowd.

Making sure that the membrane to the in-between place was properly sealed brought an end to the invasion, and as a consequence, there never was a second wave.

Daisy's picture would be in all the papers the next day if the amount of flash photography that was taking place had anything to do with it, so she intervened just a little, and none of the photographers seemed to be able to get the focus right. A huge crowd of reporters were clamouring for her story, but as she turned to walk quickly home, they found that for some strange reason, they didn't want to follow her anyway. It was several miles back to Daisy's house, so as soon as she was sure that no one could see her, she teleported the rest of the way into her bedroom.

Bishop's Ashton soon discovered that losing all of its road signs made absolutely no difference to the traffic, so they were never replaced and a campaign of civil disobedience eventually stopped the ministry of transport's efforts to do it for them.

Bruce just harrumphed, looked at Daisy and thought, "*I told you it would be a disaster.*"

End of excerpt